W9-DDD-865

The Men's Breakfast

19 NEW STORIES
FROM CAPE BRETON ISLAND

THESE TERRIFIC STORIES confirm Cape Breton Island's place on the map of exceptional Canadian fiction. The 19 stories in *The Men's Breakfast* range from the wildly comic to fragile magic, from brutal moments masterfully told to the aching heart of human relationship.

Some of these writers have achieved a bit of fame, others will be happy discoveries—and all are worth reading in this entertaining and thought-provoking book that has been built to last, to be returned to, and to share.

This one is for

Octavia and Dziko

The Men's Breakfast

19 NEW STORIES
FROM CAPE BRETON ISLAND

Edited with an Introduction by
Ronald Caplan

Breton Books

The Men's Breakfast compilation © 2011 Breton Books
All rights for the individual stories belong to the authors.

Front Cover photo: Ronald Caplan. Author photos: Russell Colman
by Carol Kennedy. Maureen Hull by David Hardy. Teresa O'Brien and
Stewart Donovan by Ronald Caplan. Joyce Rankin by Blaine Aitkens.
Dave Doucette and D.C. Troicuk courtesy Cape Breton University Press.
"*Land War*" first appeared in *The Nashwaak Review*. "Snowmobile An-
gel" is from the book *White Eyes*. "Jarvis" was originally published in *The
Fiddlehead*.

Editor: Ronald Caplan
Production Assistant: Bonnie Thompson
Layout: Fader Communications

We acknowledge the support of
the Canada Council for the Arts
for our publishing program.

Canada Council   Conseil des Arts
for the Arts   du Canada

We also acknowledge support from Cultural Affairs,
Nova Scotia Department of
Communities, Culture & Heritage.

NOVA SCOTIA
Communities, Culture and Heritage

We acknowledge the financial support of the
Government of Canada through the Canada Book
Fund for our publishing activities.

Canadä

Library and Archives Canada Cataloguing in Publication

The men's breakfast : 19 new stories from Cape Breton
Island / edited with an introduction by Ronald Caplan.

ISBN 978-1-926908-08-3

1. Short stories, Canadian (English)--Nova Scotia--Cape
Breton Island. 2. Canadian fiction (English)--21st century.
I. Caplan, Ronald, 1942-

PS8329.5.C36M46 2011   C813'.010897169   C2011-906623-8

Printed in Canada

FSC
www.fsc.org
MIX
Paper from
responsible sources
FSC® C011825

Contents

*I*ntroduction

I ATTENDED A MEN'S BREAKFAST in the basement of a local church hall and was struck by the coming together and details of a morning that seemed without any agenda, no designated speaker, nothing presented for common discussion, not even a prayer. It was just a morning of good food—bacon, eggs over, fried potatoes, orange juice, toast and coffee—and everyone's obvious desire to be part of that morning. The cook had been there since the wee hours preparing about fifty meals without knowing how many people would come, and wanting to have everything hot and ready to serve. And "serve" is the right word. Quite formally, proudly, plateful after plateful, the food was brought out by volunteers. But leading up to the meal, there was a period of greeting among those who showed up that day—a hello, a handshake, perhaps some teasing about work, a bit about their travels—the men settling into chairs on both sides of a long table, set for breakfast. Talk never stopped. And this has been the format for over twenty years, put on hold only during the period when the church was raised to make the basement larger for use for banquets, meetings and, of course, the Men's Breakfast.

A kind of tapestry was woven by those who were there. All in all, it was warm, satisfying and refreshing. It made that term—"The Men's Breakfast"—stay with me through days that followed, and seemed an event that might be honoured by using it as a title for this collection of new Cape Breton fiction. Simple as that.

CAPE BRETON SEEMS TO HAVE BECOME a kind of wellspring for award-winning and much-nominated writing in fiction, including the three-time winner of the Dartmouth Book Award, Beatrice Mac-Neil, the Giller Prize winner Linden MacIntyre and recently nominated novelist Lynn Coady, and—of course—Alistair MacLeod's win of the International IMPAC Dublin Literary Award. Pretty interesting for one small island. The world knows about our Sheldon Currie, D. R. MacDonald, Ann-Marie MacDonald, and Frank Macdonald—and I'll just arbitrarily stop there. This book grew out of wondering what's next, what's coming in fiction from Cape Breton. Some of the writers in *The Men's Breakfast* are just breaking out into wider fame, while most will be happy discoveries. In the end, they make a mix that doesn't come under a single genre or heading but certainly makes for good reading, good company. And remarkably, this is only nineteen of the writers who might have been included.

The Men's Breakfast grew out of my desire to locate some of the best newer Cape Breton writers, to discover the substance and timbre of their work, whether or not they lived here or wrote about the island. I was looking for short stories but I soon found portions of novels-in-progress by Joyce Rankin, Phonse Jessome, Maureen Hull, Brian Tucker, and Stewart Donovan that can neatly stand alone. I also found the most fragile magic delivered out of the hands of Russell Colman and Tim Vassallo, and some remarkable brute force masterfully carved by Paul MacDougall and Victor Sakalauskas. There is much that is finest about human relationship: a hard-bitten father's affection for his wayward son, a teenage youth caregiving for a disabled woman, four somewhat kooky apartment-dwellers on a road trip to a funeral.

Reading our way toward this book, we found entertainment and challenge, and perhaps a more worldly fiction than I might first have guessed. In the end, much like the Men's Breakfast I was lucky enough to attend, it is held together by the need to nourish one another and to share our stories.

Besides the team of First Readers, I want especially to thank Douglas Arthur Brown for his help in locating Cape Breton writers I might not otherwise have found; his was a generous insistence on our taking a look at good writers who may not yet have achieved any fame, and whom I might have missed. And to Sharon Hope Irwin, a vital and careful reader, who consistently brought more to this little adventure, and to my life, than I dared hope to receive.

—Ronald Caplan
Wreck Cove
Cape Breton Island

*H*ockey *N*ight
in *C*ape *B*reton

TIM VASSALLO

Oh, the good old hockey game
Is the best game you can name;
And the best game you can name
Is the good old hockey game!
—from "The Hockey Song"
by Stompin' Tom Connors

Radiances know him. Grown lighter
than breath, he is set free
in our remembering. Grown brighter...
—from "Three Elegiac Poems"
by Wendell Berry

"*H*OCKEY NIGHT IN CANADA" CAME ON the air in 1952. It was probably 1972 when it became part of my world. As a young kid, I thought it was "Hockey Night in Cape Breton," because every single TV set on the island was fixed on CBC. There were towns that had sewer lines break due to the simultaneous flushing of toilets during commercials. Saturday night *was* hockey night in Cape Breton. I used to fear seeing my grandfather falling through his floor and, consequently, my basement ceiling on Saturday nights after a Habs goal. I had witnessed his displays of loyalty—my grandfather jumping to his feet and smacking his huge hands together—witnessed that enough times to know my fear was not unfounded. Big Joe went about six-foot-four and carried

1

two-twenty like no other man. He could descend stairs without one scuff or creak. But when the game was on and Montreal was playing—look out! He went through a chair a season, I'm pretty sure, and scared Nana senseless every time that red light lit up.

"That man!" That would be the extent of her protest or, maybe, deliberately making the tea too hot at snack time.

I spent four or five years of only getting to watch the first two periods of the game and then trying to decipher those bangs and thumps on the ceiling, listening for the secrets hidden within them. Often, I would replay highlights from my memory befitting what the thumps might reveal: a fight, a goal, or a particularly bad call. I would also picture my grandfather standing straight up and clapping.

Even today, nearly four decades after, I can still remember that electric feeling that ran through my body the first night I watched an entire game. I was allowed in the den from pre-game to the three stars. I felt like I was moving past some barrier that separates little boys from men. My grandfather sat in his chair, ready for a quick dismount, and I sat next to him on the couch watching both the game and my grandfather for the cues, like at church. Stand when they stand and sit when they sit; hold your hand over your heart when that anthem is sung.

As time moved on, I would only watch part of the game with my grandfather and then, after the snack, go downstairs to our apartment and finish the game there. Still listening to the ceiling to see if the old fella agreed with the three stars.

The changes happen so quickly. Being right at the core, you miss the evolution. Just a couple of years ago I was dying to be upstairs with him, watching the game, but now I was only performing a duty. The game has three periods and I had just finished the first one.

LIFE ROLLS ON, as we all know, regardless of our ability to grasp it; the concept and the reality of time elude most of us. My grandfather was ageless for nearly ten years until, while being AWOL from university, I saw him as an old man for the first time. He moved more slowly and spoke about the past as if it were the present. He still loved hockey but now he would watch it with the sound off.

"That Dick Irwin gets my goat. If silence is golden then he's tin, for Christ's sake!"

During our regular but not frequent phone calls, we would talk about lots of things but we'd end with hockey. He had all but given up on the players of the day, preferring to talk about Beliveau or the Richard brothers. The salaries and the attitude turned him sour, and he'd often say, "There's boys who played senior hockey here in Cape Breton during the Fifties who could easily make the NHL today with its—what is it now?—forty teams, and back then the boys playin' pro only got paid an honest wage for their hard work!"

Somewhere around this part of our relationship, we moved past the second period and on to the third. The final period without overtime or—another thorn in the old guy's side—shootouts to do the deciding. Old players retire and the ones who replace them act as though no one has played the game before them. The man and the boy intersect and move in opposite directions but, somehow, end up in the same place.

IT WAS A STRANGE COINCIDENCE that I decided to move home during that final winter. I had been working out west, in a tourist town, and I felt that I had to escape. I had had all I could take. So I decided to drive home to Cape Breton and realized that I had made a terrible mistake around Brooks, Alberta. That drive was like no other, since or before. Seven days of the crappiest weather this side of the Great Slave Lake. As I made my way down the T-Can towards my island, all I could think of was Big Joe.

Upon arrival, the old fella looked thin and frail. Still, his handshake felt like a vise-grip; he would stare down at you and smirk all the while. We sat there in the den of his new place. He had moved while I was out west. I looked around at all the photos and plaques and, over in the far corner, the box of bowling trophies that once had been on full display. The room was in the basement, so it smelled of basement, of old stuff and mildew. Sitting in his new recliner, he stared at the pictures on the wall and his eyes grew wet. His hands still looked like hammers as they rested on his knees.

Later that same week, he phoned me to see if I'd go out to the country with him. When he was well, he'd go out to see the cousins in Big Pond at least once a month. I showed up at his house, and the driveway and front step were already shoveled. Inside, my grandfather was trying to pull off his snowboots, sitting awkwardly on the hall chair.

"Come here and give us a hand, boy!"

So, there I was crouched down, pulling off the cranky old bugger's boots as he cursed them hell, west, and crooked.

"They call this waterproof?"

He began to make a big scene of wringing his socks onto the sopping doormat. He was nothing if not funny. He was on the brink of a lecture about the shoddy workmanship of today. In his mind, the death of the unions was the death of workmanship, maybe even of pride itself.

He was off in his bedroom to change but was still going on about something. As he emerged from his room all I could hear was himself, voice at full throttle, belting out "I'll Take You Home Again, Kathleen." The small hallway was full of his baritone and I was awash with pride. I could watch him for hours, regardless of his activity, just being Big Joe.

"Come here, boy, tie me shoes up before I walk outa here on me sock feet."

As I was, once again, genuflecting before the old fella, I kept having flashes of the North Sydney Forum and school skating, replete with the smell of cold, stale air. The old fella would tie every single kid's skates just because he liked to tie skates. I looked up at him as I was finishing his laces and he looked like he was sleeping. I felt as if the cycle of life had passed a special and, simultaneously sad, point on its journey.

AFTER THE DRIVE BACK FROM THE COUNTRY, I went to my buddy's house to pick up the smelts for that night's supper. My grandfather had to be fed by five o'clock or else fed with a long stick, and it was past that time. I was in the kitchen, doing up the smelts and new potatoes, when I heard him fall. When I got to his room he was already on his knees trying to stand up.

"Papa, stay down. I'll call 911."

"No, boy, for Christ's sake, the ambulance will come rippin' up the street with its siren going off."

He was in real pain and it hurt me to see that. I laid the phone down and went over beside him. Minutes later, I was able to help him into the chair. He sat there like an aging pope with his white hands splayed out on the arm of the chair.

"Turn on the TV, boy!"

I went to the kitchen to get his plate and returned to see him pointing at the TV.

"Look, the Habs are playing Toronto. Toronto better call bloody 911!"

We sat there, watching the game and eating the smelts or, as the old fella loved to say, a mess of smelts. The new potatoes tasted like none before and the room was filled with smells of my past. I made the supper tea and found some cookies in the cupboard to give him as dessert.

He poured his tea into the saucer and proceeded to sip it slowly.

"An old habit." He smiled at me and his eyes had that glint of old.

I watched him more than the game. This time, the clues I

was searching for were much different from before. He just sat there, smiling.

MY GRANDFATHER ATE HIS LAST MORTAL MEAL as Montreal beat Toronto 3-1.

If you look at my life in small sections, this part offers up the template that I used to build my life. One day in his presence and a person would be left with a week of stories. Hockey was only one of our shared passions but it was the first.

The third period of the game was the saddest of all. The end came without a whistle or a horn; the time elapsed with a single breath that was never exhaled. The man who wrote the blueprint for the man I was trying to become was gone. I was lost and the game was over.

Once, as we drove up Ashby Road, I noted how many people waved at him. He would nod regally and smile. I questioned him on why he wasn't the mayor of Sydney.

"Why would I want that job?" he snapped. "Then no one would wave at me!"

Cut the Devil's Throat

JOYCE RANKIN

I WALK IN THE DOOR and flip on the ovens and the grills. I start traying bacon and sausage, mix up pancake batter, take the eggs and the butter out of the walk-in, get potatoes out for home fries, lay out loaves of bread, take the trays of bacon out of the oven and put more in, whisk eggs for French toast, slice ham and grate cheese, dice ham and onions and slice mushrooms for omelets, take the next two trays of bacon out, place stacks of breakfast plates and side plates near the grill, take the sausages out of the oven and slide them off the tray and into the chafing dish beside the grill. I slice some oranges for garnish and pinch off the prettiest sprigs of parsley, then take the third tray of bacon out and pile the slices neatly with the rest, like cordwood piled by the roadside. The trick is to set up your grill and your counter so that you have everything as near to hand as you can without making the small space too cluttered to work in.

Then the waitresses start bringing in orders, and the dance begins. I think of it as a dance for which only I can hear the music. It takes small steps on a small stage, with competent sweeping movements of the arms and finishing flourishes with the hands. There's a grace that comes from knowing what you are doing and doing it well. I spin around and reach above me without even looking, because I have carefully arranged all the tools and ingredients that I will need. I am alone in this little space and I have complete control of how I work, and what I make.

The dance is mine, and music is written in the waitresses' handwriting on the order slips, some small and neat, some large and sloppy, with all the funny abbreviations we've developed from years of working together, and notations about the customers: "toast for baby first," "extra ham in omelet," "no onions on knife." The last one is because a couple of years ago I made a sandwich for this man who has a pathological hatred of onions, and I cut it with a knife that I'd used to slice onions and neglected to wipe. Now every time Onion-Hater orders food when I'm cooking he reminds me.

You need to think ahead to the order slips down the line at the same time that you keep track of each element of the meals you are working on. Timing is everything. I make sure to have each part of the meal ready to slide neatly and precisely on the plate at the right time, and to have all the plates for each table ready together. It makes people happy when they know that someone in back, whom they can't even see, tried hard to make a nice meal for them.

I don't like it when they order eggs over hard. Eggs over hard are easy to cook and serve, but they are ugly. I take a lot of trouble to make beautiful plates of food, and I like to send them out looking pretty. Sunnyside eggs are my favourite. With their gleaming yolks yellow and round as the sun and their clean and perfect whites, they are simple and fresh and honest. Eggs over easy are subtle, neat and self-contained. Scrambled eggs are pretty and frothy and wholesome, like a little girl's Easter dress. Boiled eggs are unknowable and subject to doubt; they roll perilously around on the plate unless you restrain them in a fruit nappy or on the side, which then needs a different sort of arrangement of bacon and toast on the plate. But eggs over hard, especially when the yolk is broken and cooked hard, are just plain ugly. They are like the garbage cans and piled empty crates and broken chairs you find behind even the nicest restaurant, and seeing them spoils the beauty of the meal.

Being a parent is like that. There's the surface part that people see, bringing your kids to church on Sunday and making sure that they are clean and their hair is fixed, and that they know their prayers. Or going to Parent-Teacher Night at the school and having the teachers tell you how your child is polite to the grown-ups and kind to the other children. But there are all the things we don't talk about, like wakening in the middle of the night to clean up a child who has just thrown up all over herself and the bedclothes, and when you've got it all cleaned up she throws up again, this time all over you and her own fresh pajamas. There are the sleepless nights walking a colicky baby, when you are so tired you get disoriented and can't remember who you are but you know you have to care for this baby in your arms. There's the getting up off the couch to take a toddler outside to play in the fresh snow, even though you are dog-tired and your legs ache; or driving all over the nearby towns looking for the exact doll she asked for from Santa, so that by finding it on Christmas morning she may keep her faith in wishes and dreams.

LAST WEEK I MET THERESA MARIE, a friend of Marion's. We were at a house party and there was music. As we came up the lane someone was playing the fiddle on the deck outside and people were dancing a square set. In the kitchen Robbie set down the case of Keith's and walked over and started talking to some of his friends, sliding seamlessly into the conversation they were having, one of the men telling about his wife, who was in the other part of the house.

"Who would have thought a small woman like that could do such a thing?" and I turned my face toward them, because this sounded more interesting than the usual hockey talk.

"Lucky thing the gun was there, with the bullets handy, but still...." I was at the sink, making myself a rum and coke, searching for ice because I hate a warm drink. "What happened with the gun?" Robbie said, and I turned to listen to the man who was talking.

"The other day my wife shot a bear. We heard there was

a bear around, one of the neighbours saw him last week, and I saw where berries were torn off the chokecherry bushes. Up higher than I could reach, so I knew it had to be big, but that was down in the lower field near the river. I never thought he'd come to the house."

"Strange for a bear to come so close to the house," one of the men agreed, and they were heading toward a discussion of bears in general and other bears that had been around.

"Where was the gun?" I interrupted. "Did she have any warning? What did she do?"

"Ask her yourself, she's over there." And I walked over to the woman he pointed out.

She was a small woman, not especially athletic-looking. She seemed like a person who wouldn't have patience for pretence or self-pity. A get-it-done kind of manner about her.

"WELL, I WAS HOME ALONE, waiting for the little ones to get off the bus at the end of the lane. When the bear came into the yard and started sniffing around, I got worried. I knew the little ones would soon be coming down the lane and across the yard right where he was. I got the gun out from under our bed. We have a twenty-two that we keep for when an animal needs to be shot for mercy, or for meat. I figured I'd fire a shot in the air to scare him off.

"The house was quiet, but in the porch I could smell the two big bushel baskets of apples I picked the day before to make sauce and jelly. He must have smelled them too, because he came snuffling up into the porch. He put his face up to the screen door to the kitchen and I could see his eyes looking right at me. He smelled hairy and musky and gamey, not like any of our own farm animals.

"Then there was the dragging metal sound of the school bus brakes and the whoosh and flap of the big door opening and closing. I heard Malcolm's voice teasing his sister and her voice answering. The bear turned his head and you could see he heard them too. His shoulders turned and I could see his profile against the bright blue

sky so I raised the gun and shot him in the side of the head.

"He jumped a bit but kept on turning, and he went down the two low steps back into the yard, right toward my kids. I saw them coming, running down the lane, you could see bright red and green jackets against the tan of the lane. He turned and he was loping toward them, his arse-end very big and powerful. So I kicked open the screen door and went after him. I stopped and steadied the gun and I waited til his head went up and I aimed for the back of it, got two shots, and he stumbled. I ran a bit closer, and that time I shot him in the neck and he went down.

"I walked up to him, carefully, and looked over to where the children were standing very quiet at the edge of the yard, only a hundred feet away. They were holding each other's hands and watching me. I told them to run inside and they went. The bear was lying at my feet. I could feel the heat off him and he smelled very strong, kind of wild and dangerous. I said, 'You bastard,' and I shot him in the head again, to be sure. Then I went inside to the kids.

"When I got to the kitchen I could feel my stomach rippling and my heart beating fast and high in my chest. My legs got weak, and I sat on the couch with the kids, one hand on each of their shoulders, holding on so tight they squirmed. Then I called Allan at work and told him, but he couldn't leave, so I called Jamie next door and he came to look. I stood in the kitchen and watched him. He stood there for a minute and then turned and left. He came back with the tractor to pull the carcass out of sight behind the barn so I wouldn't have to look at it. A man from Natural Resources came, and after that Allan skinned it and took it to get it dressed, because he says that no one he knows has a bearskin in the living room, especially one they shot themselves. But I told him I won't have that thing in the house."

BY THE TIME SHE'D FINISHED telling the story, five or six women were standing listening. Some, like me, were nodding in approval as if to say, "Yes, you did the right thing." And for a few minutes there was a pause in the conversation, as if we were each weighing our inner selves, asking ourselves the question, "Could I do the same?"

But a couple of the others were looking at her with a kind of baffled fascination, as if she was both greater and lesser than themselves. As if she was put by this act in another category of women, capable of things they themselves were not. But in a way they seemed to feel slightly superior, as if the fact that they had never found themselves in such a situation was a tribute to their own superiority and good judgment, rather than the sheer good fortune that gives us so much of the best parts of our lives. No mother wants to think of the bad things that can happen to their child, so we all try to pretend something so dangerous could never happen to us. As if by protesting that we could never cope with that, we are insuring that it will not happen to us.

But I wanted to say, "No, wake up and look at yourselves. Is there any of you who wouldn't do the same in the same circumstances? That's what a mother would do. That's her job."

The men were standing over by the sink, and I went to get Theresa Marie and myself a drink. Theresa Marie's husband had left the group, and the rest of them were referring back to what she'd done. They seemed amazed, and a little embarrassed, and I wanted to say to them, "It was what she needed to do," and ask them "Why are you so surprised?" but I said nothing and went to watch the dancers.

I REMEMBER WHEN WE WERE VERY LITTLE, at home, the times that my father had gone away to work in the mines. My mother spent the winter on the farm with young children, the oldest thirteen and three preschoolers. A coal furnace to be stoked, and a woodstove for cooking, and cows to be fed and watered and milked, and pigs and hens to be fed, eggs to be gathered, horses to be fed and watered.

That fall he and the older children had dug the potatoes and laid them in the vegetable cellar. He butchered a cow, and he and my mother cut and wrapped the carcass to put into the salt barrel for the winter. The wood for the stove was cut and blocked and split, there was a full barrel of flour and bins of vegetables that we'd grown. Potatoes and turnips and carrots to last till spring. Cabbage and apples, too, but they didn't last the winter and would be used up by Christmas. But there were things they could not make for themselves; tea, sugar, molasses, salt, oatmeal, and a few things like that. And yeast. Cake yeast that came in neat one-inch cubes from the store; she needed that for making bread. Twice a week, sometimes three times, she made a batch of eight loaves. We toasted it on a wire rack over the wood fire and ate it with butter. We ate it spread with molasses for dessert, we had it with stew and gravy, and we had it for a snack.

When everything was set my father took the train to North Ontario, to Elliott Lake, to work in a mining camp for what was very big money to us. And my mother stayed at home to mind the farm. Everyone thinks there's nothing to do on a farm in the winter, but if you have animals, there's always something to be done. In winter they need to be fed and watered, there's manure to be shoveled and cows to be milked and much more.

Even the washing was hard. She had to haul water from the river to wash. She would wait until night came and the children were sleeping to start carrying the buckets of water. Except in mid-summer the water was always very cold, because it came from ice that melted from the top of the mountain. So by bringing the water into the kitchen the night before, it would come to room temperature and make it easier for her to heat it for washing.

She managed the work of the farm, with help from the children, of course. At that time, children were used to lots of chores, and we were all used to farm work. But we were eight girls and two boys. The oldest was thirteen. The boy, my brother James, was only two. I was not born yet. That's why there's a space between James and Bernadette, because Daddy was away that year. And that's where Bernadette got her name. Once he started sending money home we were able to go to the movies at the village hall on Sunday evenings, and that spring they showed *Bernadette of Lourdes*. That movie was inspirational and made for families to watch together. It was very popular at the time in small villages like ours, and so a whole cohort of little Scotch-Catholic Bernadettes were named.

But right after my father left, before he managed to send any money home, there was almost none at all, because it took pretty much all they had left to buy the ticket and give him a little stake to live on until he got working and got paid. But there were a few things she needed to buy: soap, and tea, and molasses, and scribblers for the kids in school.

There were two stores in the village. One was the co-op store, and the other was the old general merchant store. In the next village there was another smaller general store. Sometimes we shopped at the co-op store, because my grandfather had been one of the founders, and my father supported the co-op movement for the same reason he voted Liberal and went to the Catholic church; it was part of him. But the co-op store didn't give credit, so there were times when we couldn't shop there. Then my mother went to her cousin's general store. That fall, she couldn't go to her cousin's store because we had no more credit there, so she went to another little store in the next village, though she was almost at her limit there too.

It was snowing, and the tires on the old truck were bald. She went and bought an order of groceries on credit there, knowing it was her last, and that it'd have to do until the money came. She took Jessie Anne with her, and for a treat they bought a bag of hard candy, those glossy nuggets of green and yellow and orange mixed with the red-and-white striped ones. As we passed around the bag of candy, savouring the sweetness and rolling them around in our mouths, she finished unpacking the bags and realized she had forgotten to buy bread yeast. With no yeast we'd have no bread, and bread was the filler that stretched the meals to fill those growing children. To be without bread would be unimaginable.

It kept her awake that night, worrying over where she'd get the few cents to buy it. And in the morning as she stirred porridge in the heavy pot, she tried to think if she had any money at all tucked away. After the older children had left for school and the milk had been strained and the dishes done, she started to look.

First she said a prayer to St. Anthony, the patron saint of lost things. Then, methodically, she went through the house, searching through the clutter on the kitchen shelves, in the corners of her purse and the pockets of her clothes, through the top drawer of her dresser where things from pockets accumulated, through the pockets of my father's clothes that hung in the closets, anywhere a spare penny could turn up.

She found a few pennies, then a nickel, then a penny here and a penny there (one lodged sideways in a crack in the floorboards in the living room), until she had almost what she needed, but not quite. Later that day, as she was shoveling the ashes out of the furnace in the basement, she saw the flash of something round among the cinders and ashes, saw a copper penny, smudged and darkened, but still legal tender. She sifted through the rest of the ashes and found two more. One more than she needed. She cleaned them up and when Jessie Anne came from school, she sent her tramping through the field to her cousin's store with cash, the coins she had gathered, to buy yeast. And first thing the next morning she set bread to feed the children. And said a little prayer of thanks to St. Anthony.

The Drunk Tank

BRIAN TUCKER

THEY CATCH ME "DRUNK AND DISORDERLY" and toss me in the back of their Paddy Wagon. The cop that pushes me into the back is overweight and his hand on the back of my neck is slick with fat wetness. When he squeezes himself into the passenger side, the Paddy Wagon dips about a foot to the right.

"What's your name?" he asks me, breathing hard.

"John."

"With an H?"

"Yeah."

"What's your last name?"

"Roach."

"And how old are you John Roach?"

"Sixteen next month."

"So you're only fifteen then?"

"Yeah."

"A little young to be drunk on the street and acting the fool, don't you think?"

"No."

"What?"

"Yes."

"What's your father's name?"

"His name is John too. I'm named after him."

"Big John Roach is your father?" The fat cop laughs, nudges his partner next to him. "Like father like son, eh?"

The fat cop's remark sends drunken adrenaline all through me. "And is your da a fat, sweaty pig like you?" I ask, kicking the back of the seat.

The fat cop turns to face me. "Watch your fuckin' mouth, son. I'm warnin' ya."

"You watch it," I say, spitting on the glass partition in front of his face.

"That just cost you a night in the tank, kid," he says. "We were going to take you home but now it's the drunk tank for you." The fat cop laughs again. "Swing it around, Gerald," he says to his partner behind the wheel. "We're going back to the station."

"You sure about this, Dave?" Officer Gerald asks. "We got Frankie Arsenault in there."

"Yeah, so?"

"You can't put him in there with the likes of Frankie Arsenault, Dave. He'll eat him alive."

"Yes, I can," the fat cop says. "There's no law says I can't."

THE DRUNK TANK IS IN THE BACK of the station. It's a single cell behind a heavy metal door. The fat cop pats me down and takes my shoelaces. When I ask why, he tells me it's so I won't hang myself with them.

"People hang themselves with shoelaces?"

The fat cop slides the door open for me. "Alright, in ya go."

I step into the cell and he slams the door behind me.

The sound of it sobers me up on the spot.

"Got a friend for ya here, Frankie," the fat cop says. "You two got a lot in common. He thinks he's a tough guy too."

The cell has two narrow cots on each side. Sitting on one of them is the scariest looking man I've ever seen. His hair is long,

17

stringy, and tied back in a ponytail. He's wearing a ripped and dirty Harley-Davidson T-shirt, and both of his arms are loaded with the type of tattoos you receive in prison.

"Well," the fat cop says. "I've got paperwork. I'll leave you two to get acquainted."

The fat cop leaves the room whistling a happy tune.

Frankie is staring at me with a set of cold dead eyes.

I look down at my shoes with no laces.

"Hey.... You a tough guy?"

I shake my head no.

Frankie stands up.

"You a tough guy or what?"

"No. I'm not a tough guy."

"Cop said you was a tough guy." Frankie starts walking across the cell. He has a vicious sneer on his face. I can tell he wants to fuck with me, not because he hates me but just for something to do. "Why would he say you was tough if you ain't tough, huh?"

My mind races for a good answer—something cool and witty that will make him like me and not want to hurt me—but I can't think of anything but the truth. "He just said that because I wouldn't take any shit off him," I say. "He threw me in here with you to teach me a lesson. He wants you to do his dirty work for him."

Frankie grunts and shakes his head in disgust. "Fuckin' pigs," he says, spitting on the concrete floor. "They're all the same."

Frankie returns to his cot, stretches out, and doesn't look my way again.

AN HOUR OR SO LATER they come and get me. The fat cop looks disappointed to see me all in one piece. Officer Gerald, standing behind him, sighs with relief and gives me a sly smile. I like Officer Gerald, he's one of those rare oxymoronic types: A likeable cop.

"On your feet, Little John," the fat cop says. "Your dad's here for you."

"My da?"

"Yes."

The fat cop opens the door. "Come on! You comin' or not?"

I stand up but I don't go for the door. I walk over to Frankie's cot instead. "It was nice to meet you, Frankie," I say, holding out my hand. "Good luck to ya."

Frankie looks suspiciously at my hand and for a second it looks like he's not going to shake it. Then he laughs and grabs my thumb, then he hooks my fingers, and then he makes a fist and we bang knuckles. "You're alright, kid," he says. "Take it easy."

I walk out of there with extra swagger, past the fat cop and into the receiving area. Da is there. He looks tired and scared, and maybe a little drunk himself.

His face lights up when he sees me.

"You okay?"

"Yeah, I'm okay."

"Nobody raped you in there, did they?"

"*What?* Fuck off, Da!"

"You got that 'just been raped' look on your face."

"Don't start, Da...."

Da turns to the fat cop. "It wasn't you who raped him was it?"

"It most certainly wasn't...."

"'Cause you look like a rapist if I ever saw one, you fat pile of shit." Da walks over to the fat cop and shoves a finger at his fat cop face. "You ever put my fifteen-year-old kid in here again without calling me first and I'll have you fired. I could do it right now if I wanted. And I'd put it in the paper how you abused my boy here in horrible ways. I don't care if it's the truth or not. *I'LL FUCKIN' RUIN YA!*" Da pulls back a fist and makes like he's gonna hit him. "You better hope I don't see ya somewhere without that badge, you fat fuck!"

Da turns around and storms out, slamming the door behind him. The fat cop looks terrified. He backs from the room, shaking his head and babbling something about paperwork.

When he's gone, Officer Gerald calls me over and hands me a big envelope with my stuff in it. "It was me who called your dad," he says. "I didn't want to put you in there in the first place."

"I know," I say. "It's okay."

"Not all cops are like Dave, you know?"

"Oh, I know," I say.

"No really. We're not."

"I believe you," I say.

Officer Gerald leans over, puts his hand by his mouth like he's going to tell me a secret. "Can you tell your dad? I don't want any trouble from him."

"Don't worry," I say. "His bark is worse than his bite."

"I doubt that," Officer Gerald says.

Da is back in the door. "Shake a leg, stupid!" he bellows at me. "Or you'll be walking home!"

IT MUST HAVE RAINED while I was in the drunk tank. Plummer Avenue is wet and there's a misty nimbus around the streetlamps. Da has the windows rolled down a few inches and flecks of rainwater spit in at me through the open window.

"Ya hungry?"

"Starved but I don't think anything is open."

"I saw a chip van up by the taxi stand. You wanna hotdog or something?"

"Yeah, Da. Thanks."

"Don't mention it."

"Not just for the hotdog."

Da looks over at me. "I know," he says. "But let's not make this a regular thing, okay?"

"Okay," I say.

Da lights up a cigarette. The smell of tobacco fills the car and mixes with the smell of the rain.

"I did the same thing when I was about your age." Da winds down his window all the way so the smoke will go out. "But your Grandpa Wade wasn't nice about it like me."

"What did he do?"

"Never mind." Da takes a long drag off his smoke, flicks the ash out the window. "Just be glad I'm not him."

"I don't remember much about him."

"You were what when he died? Five or six?"

"Six, I think. What was he like?"

Da doesn't say anything for a while and then he says, "He was a hard-working guy who liked to drink too much." Da doesn't say anything else about it because he isn't drinking. When he's drinking and Uncle Ben is over, it's a different story. I wouldn't know anything about Grandpa Wade if it wasn't for those wild drunken stories. The kind of stories you end up telling to your own kids so they'll know where they came from and what they have to live up to.

"There's the chip van," Da says. "Good—it's still open."

The chip van is more of a camper than a van. There's a window in the side lit up and glowing so sweet you'd swear Jesus himself was in there. There's a hand-painted menu on the side and a shelf with condiments and napkins. The breeze that enters the car is hot and greasy and smells like propane-fried onions.

My stomach grumbles and growls.

"Was that your stomach?" Da asks.

"Yeah."

"Good, for a second I thought it was the apocalypse. What do you want to eat?"

"Can I get two hotdogs, Da? I'm really hungry."

"What do you want on them?"

I think about it. "Mustard, sauerkraut, and onions."

"When you start liking onions, boy?"

"Just now, I think."

Da laughs. "Be back in a sec."

Da gets out of the car and makes his way to the window. Seeing him up there makes me think of all the times we went to Dominion Beach. We used to go every Sunday. Da and I would horse around in the surf and build sand castles from buckets while Ma sat on a towel all covered up reading a book. Da would yell at her to get off her arse and Ma would yell right back, both of them fearless about what the world thought of them.

After, when it was time to go home, we'd stop and get hotdogs at a chip van and then we'd speed along the coast with all the windows down. The hot summer wind blowing wildly through our hair, drowning out our voices, and drying the wet sand on our feet.

Another car pulls in beside us and then another car pulls in beside them. They have their windows down and I can hear music from their radios. They seem to know Da and they honk and wave to him as he walks by.

"Here's your dogs," Da says, handing me a cardboard box with two hotdogs in it. "I had to put the mustard and kraut on myself. Hope it's the way ya like it."

"Looks great, Da," I say. "Aren't you having anything?"

"I ain't that hungry."

"You can have one of mine," I say. "I doubt I could eat two anyway."

My stomach growls again, as if in protest.

"Your gut is telling me something different," Da says, laughing. "Go ahead, boy. Dig in. There's nothing like a couple of dogs after a good night of drinking."

I dig in. Da is right. It's miraculous.

*H*eading *H*ome

DAVE DOUCETTE

*B*IG TRUCKS MUST SLOW DOWN when they reach me. I am in their way. Their frustration is shown with their move-the-hell-over! end-of-the-world-coming! horn blasting. "Get off the road! Even we trucks cannot see over that big bed!"And so I say out into my car, eyes on the side mirrors: "Go by me then!" If I could speed up I would rip down this road at a hundred and eighty, but eighty is my maximum. And yes I do know that this is the Trans-Canada Highway. I *have* pulled off the road, frequently. But what are they thinking as they go past, those big trucks, and now these smaller cars? Something like, God in heaven, thank you I am not that fellow. Is he in poverty? Or is he so wretchedly mean and ignorant that he doesn't understand that there are people and methods to move things properly? Are we seeing the result of some domestic dispute? Look at that towering bed as the snow and the wind and rain of April catch at it. Tied up with ropes, it is a pretty poor match for the forces it faces. Watch how that dirty soaked end of a blanket underneath it all—how it is undermined and flaps and twists together with a freed section of the green tarp that binds it all. Let us pass. Let us pass for Jesus' sake! Man on the road, you remind us of too many things. And inside the car there, look, his things are jammed up solid—see, a boot, look, a cast-iron frying pan up against the glass. And here he is at last. Man alone. But he's waving and smiling at us, oblivious to all that is practical. He looks to be enjoying the load he's got, heading north with all his junk.

Another car passes me. Yes, it is junk, and yes, praise God that it is not any of you in this little car that rises from the pavement of this miserable highway where more cars like yours go freely past. I switch my windshield wipers to maximum. There's another truck horn blast. Fuck. But there is no alternative but to motor on.

Night on the road approaches with its sense of futility. I am in Cape Breton, now driving through an Indian reservation—and all at once know that I do not have it in me to drive up my hill tonight, to enter all its cold lumber. The disturbance of wind ends and the car and bed ride more smoothly. Also there is less traffic. Slowly the snow drops, unbothered. My speedometer says seventy then drops down to nothing as I come to stop at the public phone outside Vi's Restaurant in Whycocomagh. I get out, put in a coin and punch the numbers for my brother in Cheticamp.

"Patrick."

"Hello, Christopher."

"You alone there?"

"Sure. Why, where are you?"

"About an hour away. I was thinking of paying a visit."

"Do it."

"But stay by the phone, will you."

"I'll be here."

My brother's wife and daughter are still in Ontario. The family spends the summer here and he has come early to set up the house. He has his dog with him for company, a large brown capable one. This is a better idea. There is running water at his place, tea, and this brother likes to make soup, pea soup, I remember. And if there is no soup made I know he will let me make it. As I drive further inland across the island, traveling northwest, this idea improves to become the best thing in the world. Despite my car being asked to do extra duty, despite its nose pointing towards the mountains and the night of the northwest, three hours out of the way, nothing could be better. Patrick and I can talk the night away, can sit and look from his living room window out onto his flat property. Of course we speak a common language, the language of memory, and have plenty to say in it if we want to say it, as each is much of the other's memories. Patrick. His name alone creates countless scenes of the world shared.

I pull into his yard in the dark and shut off my engine. The car settles in the dead damp grass as if there were no longer wheels on it and the whole thing decided to bend its fore and hind legs and lie here to wait on the ground till morning. My brother comes out the door and stands under his light bulb. The lit yard shows alongside the house where the mower couldn't get the tall lifeless grasses of last year.

"Is it covered in plastic?"

He means my bed, he means everything under the large green tarp. His tone is his sincerity. He knows what it is to travel like this. Pragmatic is what he was, driving off the obvious comedy, choosing not to reply off-handedly to the outrage that was my effort to transport my stuff. The car door swings wide, my feet out on the ground, I rest a moment, the steering wheel digging into my hip. The dog comes to my hands but leaves me for the car, sniffing a back tire.

"There's no plastic, just the tarp. I'm not worried. The bed's all right."

"There's stew."

We go inside and I look down at his electric baseboard heaters. Bending to take off my footwear, I feel the heat from the heaters rise to my cheek. It is beautifully dry. Patrick waits in his kitchen. His place is one story, one bedroom, and one bathroom. This house is a simple cove but deep, one that leaves outside all the troubled waters of this night and this day and any other storms. Perhaps I have finally learned the math, and that it's important to come to others as I have tonight.

"I'm going to Ingonish tomorrow," I say. "To work on the house for the spring."

"That place must be taking its toll on you. It's too early yet to go over there. It's Siberia over there yet, wait till the weather clears up. Even I didn't expect a cold snap this late in the year."

"What's your dog's name?"

"You always ask me that. Thor."

At low but clear volume, a battery radio plays. I gave him that radio for a birthday years back. The radio also has a flashlight. In case. Patrick always tells me he has got great use out of it and that it was one of the best things he ever got. The gift hangs on a hook from the ceiling in the corner by his picture window. CBC plays. It comes in superbly on this side of the island, not so well where I'm heading. The dog Thor, who has been sitting at attention and looking up, drops to the floor. My brother passes me a hot bowl. I take the spoon and looking ahead, blow on the steam. Pieces of big carrots float on the brown surface.

Not a long time later I am on the couch. My brother is in his bedroom with the door open. He has his light on and is reading a book about a storm. I have just told him a story about two brothers who got lost in the highlands above Mabou, one got out after dusk and the other they found in the morning with such a bad fright in him that he was never the same again. I have read this in a copy of *Cape Breton's Magazine*, which I found on the arm of the couch. I don't say where the story came from. I put out the light above me.

"That so?" he calls back.

Thor is beside me and is gloriously quiet. He only moves to adjust his mouth with a smack, or to sigh. My brother is a park warden.

"We have found people like that, and there are many cases reported."

I do not reply. This is a pleasant dry place and, very tired with a strong sensible dog beside me, I experience much comfort. So much so that I don't want to change anything. Perhaps I will stay a few days.

My brother talks on and on. He switches topics and I learn about his beehives. An hour goes by before he stops.

"You awake in there?" he says.

Deep breathing is my answer. I choose not to respond.

"Bastard." That is his final word of the night. And he is right to end with it because only a bastard would fall asleep when someone else is talking to him.

Then I don't hear anything till the middle of the night when the heavy-footed dog gets up and moves around in the dark. It is as if he is searching for something. But there comes a stillness next, like before a creature urinates. The proceeding is not that but rather a munching from his food bowl. He stops a moment, perhaps checking to see that there is no other sound beyond his eating. Then he continues till he finishes, at which point I hear him go to my brother, who has told me about this—the dog likes to be thanked for eating, or to show its gratitude after a meal. The dog will go to Patrick's bed at night like this and shove his snout toward my brother's head on the pillow, and my brother must wake to pat the head. Then the dog ambles back out here and requires the same of me. It has shown an immediate fondness for me since I arrived. I know that is because his master and I have virtually the same voice. Perhaps the dog has spent the night in stereo. I believe he has chosen to remain near me because I am the quieter speaker. I pat him kindly. He falls heavily and kicks at the floor to get his back closer in against the couch.

Spirit stronger the next day, I wake with no problem. Out the picture window there appears to be no dramatic change in the weather except that the wind is gone and the snow comes in big furry flakes that stay far apart from one another.

"Are you sure you don't want to stay?" my brother asks from his bedroom door, and the truth might be that I don't want to go on.

Getting in the car, I am told to come back if it is rough on the other side. He is not working much these days and has time till the Park opens. And if he did not have time, that would still be okay anyway. I watch him go back inside his door, the dog stepping in first over his feet.

Driving the roller-coaster mountains between Cheticamp and Cape North I smell the brakes burn, especially on the second mountain where my big bed twists queerly down the sharp meanders, screwing like a barge caught in fast eddies. When I come to Cabot High School, I pull into its entrance to tighten the bed. There is now a big steel fence across the entrance to the school. Like a cage. I presume the few cars in the parking lot belong to teachers. The building appears to be vacant. But it always did. Everyone is in class. It is hard to know whether there is anything going on inside beyond this vacancy suggested from here. But it is a school and a school is a lonesome building when classes are in.

Coming through Ingonish from the north and having visited my brother in Cheticamp, I have delayed my return, have taken the long way home. A light snow with more big flakes ends in North Bay, and in the clarity of it all it feels as if it is a hundred years ago. Not a soul is out on the road. Dejected smoke comes from the chimneys I pass. And driving over North Bay Bridge, I see the swollen water below, and above the water the dark dark mud of spring. One car approaches from the south, its occupant waves. I wave back but do not make my wave in time. Looking in the rearview mirror I take note of the car. I will find out later who drives it.

O, I make it all the way up my driveway the first time. This feat alone gives me a great sense of completion. Now there is only the unpacking and the ease that comes from putting this experience behind me. The mess I've left and the cold of winter are still on the hill. Short irregularly cut boards from the last large stage of construction show through the thawing and dropping snow. Much earth from the bank behind the house has fallen. This is a broken hill which these hands and this heart have been commissioned to mend. With tears that do not leave my chest these days but sit like ice drops on a winter window, drops that must someday descend, I look around. And they sit heavier still on this day because one large ordeal ends and an even larger one begins.

I get the last items out of the car, then switch on the temporary power to the house. Hoisting my bed up to the third floor, lumbering it up over the ladder, I set it up under the south gable, under the sloping of the mountain, then cover its sides and top with the green tarps that came with its delivery. I will create a canopy bed. And soon enough I have something made that a child with the same materials would make, a child with my strength and my size.

A very cold May afternoon begins, a new month. And too early and too wrong to wrap myself in blankets and wait on the bed for the winter to be done, I begin what is before me.

There are two flatbed truckloads of spruce planks lying packed on the second floor. This is the siding for the whole house. I brought it all inside on a trip down here with my father in midwinter because I had wanted it to dry. It hasn't, and now has to go back outside, all of it.

I get three boards out and then I stop on the threshold of the hastily sawn-out hole I have in the back for an entrance. How much is in here to bring out? I'll be an old man before I get it all out, and did the weight of all this damage the floor? How many cursed times is it that I must drag things in just to drag them back out? If I did something wrong along the way in life, I am now surely paying for it. No question there. My eye catches a thick rope that last fall someone hung over a suspended beam. A discarded fishing rope, green, spiky—it hangs three or four feet at the longest end and ever so slightly moves yet it has not been touched. Some airflow must have it. Sickeningly I turn from it to wonder why I suddenly feel bad about it. I am inside taking the rope down when my neighbour Moses arrives.

"How did you know I was here, that fast?"

"Oh, give me a second.... Smoking is the first but your hill is the second thing that will kill me. I saw you coming around the harbour carrying that tower. What was it, another floor you're putting on this place?"

"No, something to sleep on."

"Well, you're not sleeping here tonight. All this can wait. Come on up, my wife is gone."

"What do you mean she is gone?"

"She took the boys into town for the night is what I mean. What do you think I mean? Come up and stay at the house to-night. You like this kind of thing, I know, but no man can stay in the likes of this. We left nature and got used to heat a long time ago. Come on."

I leave with him, and which angel it is that has just reached down to put a hand on my shoulder and ease me up with the other from out of the ditch where I lay, I don't know. Perhaps it is no angel, just a brother and a friend. Or perhaps it is myself—I am asking for help, or allowing it, which is hardly any different. I might be helping my own self up, the lone wolf, the one for whom help has been refused without a thought of concern for myself. How hard life had been till these two moments, till last evening. How much harder.

Moses is talking about not attempting the road with his car because of his shocks. The car is parked at the bottom. We tramp down to the main road through snow and mud, when I stop and do not continue.

"No, listen, not today. You go ahead. Tomorrow, Moses." He stares a moment.

"You know yourself if I wanted to I could pick you up and carry you there and make you stay." Then he twists his head and leaves. "It's up to you. Change your mind, you know where I am."

There is something I must do first, probably the hardest thing I will ever do, which is to put up one board. If I nail one board to the house, work has begun and once it has begun, the job will only have the end, to continue towards. As it is now there are the two rough points, the beginning and the doing, and the beginning is by far the harder. The job is the siding, a finish material, this six-inch spruce plank, unplaned, one inch thick—coming in eight, ten, twelve, fourteen and sixteen-foot lengths. If I get one board up, it will have become a whole different matter.

I am outside and have chosen the southeast corner, the one most open to the elements. Though the entire heaving chest of the North Atlantic blows up here, I will put one board up, the vertical corner board. The smell of the sea gets in through my nose and mouth. Everywhere is grey in the Atlantic today and a gale blows just outside Middle Head. In turn, rows of whitecaps march across to the peninsula like patterns in a shooting game at a fair. There is the expiration of something, a gust, a draft, and all the dampness of a sea comes up in the air that reaches here.

Climbing the ladder, I measure carefully where the board butts up against the eave, then retreat to make the cut with the saw. I go back up the ladder, then right back down because this cut has been wrong. Too long. All this I do once more because the next cut is also bad. Too short and the wrong angle. Spoiled boards gather at my feet. That's all right, they can be used again. Or kindling.

Biting the finger to get the glove off, I feel the board I now have in my hand to be wetter, heavier, splintery on my skin. With this bare hand I can hold the board better; but before me is its flesh and I swear on the spot that this is wrong, that neither this hand nor the other was made for any of this. Then what were they made for? Many things, not this. Only my heart was made for this. The tyrant of them all—the authority, the one most dastardly to work for. I have a heart that has got me here in this hell and abroad in other hells. But also that heart has not let me down so I should not abuse it too much. A heart that has got us in something, if abused, might not get us out and I need it to get me out. But to do so it first must begin with getting this complicated cut right now and nailing it up with these nails, these nails that I won't take into the house.

I am off square, the board is too short. More mistakes gather at my feet. Well, fuck this. I go inside out of a gust that comes right after to shake the area where I was working. Inside where the moisure is imprisoned, the building a wet ten degrees cooler. Come heart, one board. Head? Anything. Just nail something up there.

I go out and cut another. The wind having risen, I climb the ladder another time to nail in solid the first board of the year. It is up!

Out on the ground next, stepping back, I see that it is too short at the bottom and must take it down and cut another. Turning my face to the breakers way down at the sea, I watch the waves lift then crack open on this side of the gut. Here is your view, all you ever wanted. Look, look through eyelashes dripping now, and with your concern of a bare hand that you have just struck and cut while holding yet another board that gets marked with your blood. Blink away the drips. My jacket sleeves are heavy on my arms. The hair at my forehead sits in small wet tails and putting down this new board I have cut I go back inside.

No windows, a homemade opening for a door, the entire house's siding on the floor. Thousands and thousands of pieces of wood, every size and every shape strewn and piled every which way. In a type of darkness I plug in the kettle. A downpour comes. It is against the roof and comes loud in a house empty like this. I turn to watch it from the yawn of the entrance, then walk over to slide back in place the sheet of plywood I use to cover half the opening. I do this because the suggestion of light is cold.

Unplugging the kettle when it nearly reaches boiling, I go out in the rain and with my next board under an arm I climb the ladder. I don't think of having stayed with my brother now, I don't think of being near the nice fire in the finished house of a good neighbour, about talking of all things lightly. I think of nothing, which is the only true state and the way to think at such a time as this, when all has gone to hell, when you are having success with a board. Done!

Getting down off the ladder, I close my eyes hard, then look up. The corner board is up. There is just the following of this one with the next. And then the following of that.

Snowmobile Angel

LARRY GIBBONS

*L*ULU WANTED HER OWN SNOWMOBILE more than anything else. She loved moving fast. Loved watching the ground whiz underneath her feet like she was in an action cartoon. It drove her crazy watching the snowmobilers blowing by her house on their machines. Just so cool. Their drivers looking like ancient knights hidden behind snowmobile armour and wearing the coolest helmets. And today was the first snowfall of the winter and the snowmobiles were roaring and screeching around every part of Granite Cove Reserve. No siree, she wouldn't mind getting her fiery red hair into one of those helmets and blasting a few flakes into the cold winter air.

However, the only chance she had to drive one was when her Uncle Pat brought his extra one over and that wasn't near often enough. And that was only if her brother, who was fourteen and two years older than her, wasn't at home. Her uncle thought she was too young but that little Rodney twerp had his own snowmobile and he was only ten.

Last night a black cloud had clumped up from the other side of the mountains and spat out a foot of snow. Soft, cool, tempting white fluff, and what luck that this very morning her uncle had arrived in his black pickup, loaded for snowmobiling. Two shiny red snow machines in the back. He was out of his truck and roaring them down the ramp in no time. He did everything in a hurry.

"Your brother around?" Uncle Pat shouted. He always shouted and then at about every fourth vocal explosion spat out disgusting black tobacco. He said it tasted like candy. Lulu thought it smelled like bad dog breath. Her brother wasn't around. He'd gone to the city to look at new snowmobiles. Lulu was jealous about that but then again maybe she could use it sometimes.

"Your lucky day, Lulu. Do you want to go snowmobiling?" he asked. As if! Her uncle was soon giving her a quick review of how to handle the controls. He always did that and it irritated her. He never did it to her brother.

"Just go slow at first. You don't snowmobile very often so you probably need a little warm-up," he said.

Neither did her brother, and her uncle never talked to him about warm-ups.

A snowplow roared by, making snow walls along the roadside. They'd sure be fun to do a snowmobile jump over. There was already a huge one in front of Candy's house. Her house was at the end of a dead end street and Lulu could only see the second-story bedroom window of Candy's house because of the big snow pile that the snowplows had pushed there.

As she looked at Candy's house she had the funny feeling in her stomach that she sometimes got. Like her stomach was hiding a sad feeling and trying to drag her into it. It always left her with a crowded sensation in her lungs.

But she soon forgot about her weird feeling as they roared and revved their engines. She even did a few jump starts which sent her heart a-pitter-pattering to a different drumbeat. So exciting! And when they roared down the road it felt like being on a powerful stallion. She imagined she was flying through the white-shrouded world like Gluskap. It was totally exhilarating as the cold air bit at her nose and the wind sounded as excited and gleeful as she felt.

CANDY'S HOUSE WAS SHROUDED IN WHITE too but there was no merriment there. A shroud of misery and purpose.

35

Candy's mother had died of emphysema last year, and Candy's two kids had recently been removed from her care.

Earlier in the day Candy had gone outside to cut wood. Slapped the heavy red axe down on the dried birch until her right shoulder and lower back felt like they were as hot as she hoped the fire box in her stove would be. Hot as the anger and despair in her soul.

Candy had taken two painkillers. They alleviated some of the physical pain, but didn't touch the kind of pain that kept her crying and whimpering at night when the outside world seemed to be a million miles away. Two pills couldn't put a dent in that. She had other plans for how to deal with her furious grief.

Candy looked into the medicine cabinet mirror. Saw that her undiminished emotional pain had fully masked her face. Not her face anymore. Staring her down. She was gazing at a stranger who had no interest in her happiness. The bad things she had endured, which she had fought against all her life, had won. Taken her hostage. Her soul had fled into the forest to hide in its nurturing darkness and it refused to give her even a pinch of hope that it might return. So she didn't feel like a real person anymore.

She pushed more birch logs into the wood stove. Poked them into a mound. Her soul might be in the forest but her alien self was going to burn in the unwavering flames. She watched what looked like her fiery image turning into an abhorrent orange and red false face, and it was smirking. Smirk all you want, Candy thought, because her soul was waiting for her and they would be reunited once she purged this horrible intruder. The flames roared their approval as the stovepipe's thermometer headed towards the danger zone.

She tossed her newest anti-depressant prescription into the grasping fire. The fire swallowed the eucharistic sacrifice. She left the stove door open a crack to get the fire furious. Only a surge of angry hell would expunge every vestige of shame and contempt that her mind held for her. A scornful and mocking mind that roared at her goodness and was contemptuous of her having to swallow another three pills. Only for the courage did she take them because she wanted to share in the immolation. Needed to.

Candy piled logs, a wooden folding chair, her family's pictures, and all of the paintings—years of her work—around the fiery stove. Then she locked the door, prayed to Mary and Jesus, glanced up at the Last Supper picture hanging crooked above her television set, and then laid her strangeness down on the blue-cushioned couch. She stared at the nicotine-stained stucco ceiling and prayed for strength like Jesus must have prayed before he was nailed to a tree. This would be her pain. She would own it. Going to meet her soul where her abusers and her demons couldn't follow. One path taken and no choices left for others.

Soon her children would be free of this non-person and able to get on in the world without her weighing them down.

It was in the heat, the beginning stages of searing pain and the odour of free-ranging smoke that she heard the distant roar of a machine. The flame's roar and the engine's shriek sounded to Candy like a purring cat. Snuggled up next to her, its warm body spreading its heat into Candy's trembling body.

LULU HAD THE HANG OF IT. Wasn't that hard. They coasted onto the path that ran through Magic Mushroom Woods. A raven rattled a spruce tree as it lifted off a high branch and sent snow pummelling towards Lulu to splatter on her blue lightning-bolt helmet. She loved making a fresh path through the newly settled snow. So neat to know that they were the first ever, in the whole universe, to roar over this spanking new fluffy stuff.

They turned onto Macey Road. The one that was a dead end. The road that ended at Candy's small front lawn where a perfect beginner's snow mountain waited for Lulu and her stallion. She heard the funny clicking noise again when she accelerated. It seemed to have started when the snowmobile was warmed up. Probably a normal sound for this snowmobile, Lulu thought.

She gave the snowmobile a touch of gas and the clicking sounded louder. Oh well, she wouldn't go too fast. Just easy up and easy over. She did feel that weird feeling in her stomach again but it was buried by the excitement of doing a little stunt on the snowmobile. She knew Candy wouldn't care if they went over the snow mound and then around the house. Lots of kids went around Candy's house.

"Okay. Don't go too fast and we should ride right over the snow drift," Uncle Pat shouted.

Lulu revved her machine up. The trees began to slide by more quickly as she pointed her machine towards Candy's house. Uncle Pat slowed down as he got to the drift and was able to nicely make it up the slope and down and into Candy's front yard. A beautiful path for Lulu to follow.

Lulu accelerated a little more and she had only a brief second to notice that Candy's window was looking foggy and like the glass was shimmering. No more time to think about that because her machine, which had been moving super smoothly and at a manageable cruise, had suddenly accelerated, by its own lonesome, and was now gaining in speed. Which was very worrisome because Lulu hadn't tried to speed up, and when she tried to slow the snowmobile down she was shot back in her seat by another burst of acceleration which Lulu quickly realized had her going at a dangerous speed.

Lulu tried everything to slow down her machine, but just before the machine went up the snowbank she panicked and jumped off.

THE PAINKILLERS HAD MADE CANDY SLEEPY but not enough to take her mind off the anger and sadness and heat that were building up in the room. The flames had caught onto the paper. The bottom of her dining room set was smouldering.

Now every breath made her lungs feel like they were scorching inside.

She could tell that the chair leg had caught fire because she could see the flames on the ceiling eating up the chair shadow. The carpet that ran to the couch was also burning, the toxic smoke making her head feel like a lump of concrete. Her right side felt like she had a bad sunburn. She prayed for the strength to be able to withstand the pain. She needed the pain. That's why she hadn't deadened all her sensations with pills. To just overdose and not get to feel—well, that was being a non-person who couldn't even die with any kind of painful dignity. She wanted this stranger to suffer. She wanted to feel the revenge.

Candy took one last glimpse at the flames to ensure that her fire was competent to do its job, and then she closed her eyes and waited for the sacrifice to be offered. Then she'd have freedom from pain and a glorious reunion with her lost soul.

OUTSIDE, THE RIDERLESS SNOWMOBILE had launched itself into the air. At turbo speed. Its treads searching for a grip and finding it on the window ledge of Candy's living room. From its tenuous hold on the flaked green paint it shot forward, through the glass, and into the inferno as flames and cinders spread everywhere. The snowmobile ended up on its side, the front facing the tiny microwave on the kitchen shelf. Its hind end rested underneath the kitchen table while the salt shaker leaned over the ledge and poured salt into its crimped wound. The engine was still going and the belt was still turning, totally disrupting Candy's liturgical attempt at starting fresh.

Lulu's snowmobile crash, the ensuing mayhem, smoke and flames, and the general attention this drew to Candy's house was a very bad thing for Candy's plans.

Lulu thinks that both of her angels—for she believed she had two—had performed a double whammy. The one angel, Mary, had made sure that she hadn't been seriously injured, and her other angel, Joseph, had used a really intelligent way to wake Candy up from her despair.

And you know, it's hard for anybody to ignore a holy sign. Candy was not going to ignore hers. A snowmobile going through your front window while you are involved in a serious sort of soul-seeking business is definitely a sign and not only that, it's another chance.

So Candy went back to her painting. But now she paints surprises. People being surprised by God. People being surprised by angels. She gave Lulu a twenty-by-twenty-four-inch painting of an angel riding on a radiant snowmobile, the snow forming a yellow halo above the rider's head, as the snowmobile and angel are bursting through the fiery portal. Lulu has the painting hanging in her bedroom next to her white wolf picture.

Lulu was given a snowmobile by an unknown donor. It's her powerful horse and whenever she gets that funny feeling, whether she is riding on her snowmobile, driving her bike or walking, she gives an extra careful look over the place that is giving her that strange feeling and makes sure that things are okay.

Sometimes she thinks of herself as the third angel. Mary, Joseph, and Lulu.

Bon Appetit

ANGUS MACDOUGALL

"THESE PICKLED BEETS are real tasty," Stan Webster told his wife Ree.

"You had beets yesterday," Ree reminded him.

"Yeah, boiled ones," Stan replied. "I like beets, supposed to be good for you they say. This is a great lunch, hon. That ham was some good too, juicy and tender, not dry and overcooked like some people do."

Ree was short for Henrietta. She was short herself, just a shade over five feet tall. She had curly blonde hair and never seemed to stop around the kitchen.

"I think I'll go with a dish of shepherd's pie for supper," Ree promised. "You haven't seen that for a while."

"Can't wait."

Raising his 235 pounds out of his captain's chair, Stan moved away from the kitchen table towards the back porch. In his right hand he carried a mug of hot tea and in his left a fishing magazine. He wore a camouflage-coloured outfit with many pockets of different sizes and shapes. His pants were held up by a pair of wide khaki suspenders. His black leather ball cap with a Chevy decal was tilted back on his forehead.

"Put that nice thick crust on it, babe; then a bit of ketchup and we'll be all set."

He settled into a large wooden chair in the sun porch, sipping his tea and flipping through the magazine.

"Remember the last time you made shepherd's pie, I cleaned up the whole dishful. Mind you it wasn't a very big dish, but still you figured we'd have some left over to take camping. Instead I finished it off in one shot."

"You're right," Ree laughed. "It ended up we had to take some spaghetti sauce and meatballs from the freezer and thaw them out on the way to the country. Hot that day too. Same sauce recipe we got from Al the chef at Gagetown thirty years ago or more."

The Websters were a military family. Stan had served twenty-eight years in the Army, handling ordnance of various kinds. They had lived on bases all over Canada. Stan proudly wore the blue beret on UN peacekeeping tours in Cyprus and the Golan Heights. When he retired twelve years ago, the family moved back home. They bought a two-bedroom bungalow on the water in Groves Point, just a few miles from North Sydney where Stan had been raised. To top up his pension, Stan repaired lawn mowers and small appliances. He ran this business out of a barn in his backyard. He also tied fishing flies for sale. In front of their house was a neat, white handmade sign with painted red letters which read "Night Crawlers $2.00 a Dozen." In all these enterprises Stan didn't trouble his customers about taxes, which helped keep him fairly busy.

"That spaghetti dinner was some tasty too, hon," Stan said. "Things always seem to taste better in the country for some reason, I find. At least your brother Sam helped himself to a coupla' platefuls when he dropped in for supper that night. Cleaned us out of meatballs at the time too, if I'm not mistaken."

"Sam always had a pretty good appetite even when we were kids home. Of course, Mother was a great pusher of food in her day."

"You're pretty good at that yourself," Stan smiled. "'The acorn don't fall far from the tree,' as they say."

"Sam used to be strictly a meat and potatoes man for years," Ree continued. "A fish n' brewis, Jiggs-dinner eater, I'd call him. Now lately he's starting to go for all this foreign grub, Middle Eastern, Mexican, East Indian."

"Sam's got nothing on your older brother Wally though. Now there's a man who can eat! Chicken wings, Thai stuff; rabbits, eels, ducks. The gamier the better. He'll tackle just about anything from a barbeque," Stan said, with more than a touch of admiration in his voice.

"Wally claimed his first wife, that Louise one, tried to starve him to death for eight years. He's been making up for it ever since," Ree noted.

And in fact Ree's shepherd's pie made for a very successful supper. Stan had to add hardly any salt or pepper—just the aforementioned layer of ketchup.

"It's a funny thing about ketchup," Stan reflected at supper time. "You see all these yuppies sweating it out trying to come up with the perfect salmon dip, or lobster dip, or some kind of herb dip—and you know what, pet?"

"What?"

"Never saw a dip yet can hold a candle to good old Heinz ketchup, as far as I'm concerned."

"Dips aren't real food anyway," Ree frowned. "They just help pass the time as far as I can see, something else to talk about. One person trying to outdo the other. A person could crack a tooth too on some of the crackers they use to dip with—the thickness of them."

"You can say that again, dear. A person could famish relying on dips, no matter how tasty."

"Personally, I don't bother wasting time making them," Ree sniffed. "Now soup, soup is another story. Soup is different altogether."

Stan's eyes lit up.

"You make some lovely soups, dear, practically a meal by

themselves. Your beef vegetable I think is your top one. No no," he corrected himself quickly. "No, maybe your fish chowder even beats that. If chowder qualifies as a soup, that is."

"Thanks, Dad. I get lots of good comments on both. I always feel soup should be hardy, then if someone cares to fill up on it, well they can suit themselves. But if they wanna have a couple of spoonfuls just to try it, and leave plenty of room for the main course, well that's their business."

Stan listened closely, as he always did, whenever Ree gave an opinion about food and eating. They were both in their mid sixties. She was from a Polish family in Whitney Pier. She and Stan met during a dance at the old Venetian Gardens on the Esplanade. At the time Ree worked at a restaurant called the Diana Sweets on Charlotte Street. After Stan joined the Army and they were married, she never worked outside the home. She loved to cook and was very good at it. Her name Henrietta meant "little house ruler" in Polish.

"Speaking of room, Dad, you got any left for some mincemeat pie left over from the weekend?"

"Mincemeat or that blueberry'd hit the spot, lover. A little dab of cheese on the side wouldn't hurt either—just to top it off."

"You like your cheese alright. But it'll have to be that No Name brand stuff, the price a cheese these days."

"Yeah, like that Oka we'd get by the shovelful in the sergeants' mess in Petawawa. Those were the days. You couldn't cover a ten-cent stamp with what you get for five bucks these days. Don't know who buys it. Lawyers' wives, I guess."

"By the way, speaking of lawyers, did ya hear what our Winston said to Harry Melski the lawyer's mother last Saturday at our Fortieth Anniversary party?" asked Ree.

"No. I heard them all laughin' but I didn't catch it," Stan replied.

Winston, a pleasant man of thirty-two with no trace of the "army brat" in him, was their only child. He was an assistant supervisor at a call centre over in Sydney. He had been christened Winston Spencer Churchill Webster in honor of the wartime leader.

"Winston goes 'Not too much business for divorce lawyers with people like Mom and Dad around, Mrs. Melski. Your Harry'd be starvin' if everyone stayed together like them two.'

"Leave it to that Winston to get things going. Old Mrs. Melski wasn't stuck though. She says: 'Well one thing's for sure, your father doesn't look like he's starving the way your mother feeds him.'

"Winston took to the laughin'. 'Oh,' he says, 'Da only goes about 250 but no one knows for sure. He won't go near a scale. Doesn't know how to use one. The only scales he knows about are the ones on the pickled herring he puts away while he's waitin' on dinner.' That Winston's a card. I don't know what he sees in that girlfriend of his though, that Michele."

Stan was careful to say nothing more on the subject of Michele. And so, after finishing the shepherd's pie, he and Ree pored over Sobey's weekly flyer. They studied it closely, as if someone had handed them the map to Captain Kidd's treasure. They then set out for Sobey's in North Sydney, to pick up a few things and check on their lottery tickets. Before they left, Ree made sure she put on her lucky brown sweater with the St. Jude medal pinned to the collar.

"That shimmy's still there in the front end," Stan said as they drove along. "Can you feel it, babe?"

"Right. And the air conditioning isn't working smooth. And the driver's door won't shut tight; and it needs winter tires. I'll run down the whole list and save you the trouble."

"It's all true, hon," Stan laughed. "This rig's fifteen years old and besides, I noticed some rust around the rear window the other day."

"You've been campaigning harder than Obama for another

car ever since your brother-in-law Wally got his new Mazda last month."

"Doesn't have to be new. The big thing is the trunk has to be roomy and dry. I don't care if it's a Chev or a Ford or whatever. Long as we can get all our stuff in there. A few hampers; a good-sized cooler; portable barbeque; some pots and pans. I'm gonna get Ambrose Wright down at the garage to look around for us the next time he goes to the car auction up in Halifax."

Ree stayed quiet, which Stan took for the green light to call his friend Ambrose. In fact the trunk of their car resembled a traveling pantry like the mobile canteens Stan remembered from military maneuvers.

They had no luck with their lotto tickets. On their way home from shopping, they dropped by Wally's place. His shiny new Mazda sat in his driveway. Before going into the house, Stan unlocked the trunk of their car. Ree leaned in and picked up a dish of homemade perogies, one of her specialties. She also took out a plate of brownies, a thermos of coffee, and a box of Ritz crackers. All of these had been stored neatly in a large plastic container.

"Bring in a few tins of sardines why don'tcha, hon; over there in the corner next to the wheel wrench," Stan pointed. "Wally loves them for a little lunch in the evening."

"Wally! Never mind Wally! You never turned down a sardine in your whole life; you grab them."

Wally sat in his living room watching the Boston newscast. He turned the TV off right away when his sister came through the back door. He looked towards the kitchen as Ree uncovered the perogies and placed them in the microwave. Only then did Wally speak.

"Bill Davis' brother lost his job over at the drugstore. Pile of money disappeared. Mounties were called in. Drugs missing too, they say.

"Dan Walsh's mother-in-law Lena Snow was put in the

home—dementia. Cops found her at 4 a.m. trying to get into that school where she used to teach."

Stan called it the "de-briefing," the way Wally opened every conversation with all the latest bad news. Stan stared silently at the empty TV screen during this recital. Ree took a few brownies and laid them on a side plate. The microwave hummed in the background.

"Art MacDonald's son was run over in a crosswalk in Ottawa. Still in a coma; took him off life support yesterday. Just turned twenty-eight with a wife and two pre-school kids. Had a good job. Engineer with the federal government."

Stan and Ree could never figure out where Wally came up with all of this sad news. He was well into his 70s and retired from the post office. He hardly moved out of the house since his second wife Matilda died five years ago.

"Two for Barlett's, one for Pelley and Sons."

Wally had put on his bifocals and was now reading from the obituary page of the daily paper. He kept close track of how many funerals went to each of the local undertakers. "Just one for Slade's, I'm afraid. Oh, oh, look at this"—his voice rose slightly—"One...two...yep, it looks like three for Gallant's in Glace Bay." Wally let out a brief admiring whistle. "A hat trick," he said.

Stan called it the "rough box score."

"Gillis in New Waterford shut out again, I'm afraid," Wally went on. "Second time this week; none last week either." The look on his face seemed to say, "What is Gillis doing wrong? He'd better smarten up if he expects to stay in business."

"I knew old Lena Snow; used to come into the Diana Sweets for lunch quite a bit when I worked there," Ree said. "Good tipper too. Newfoundland girl. She was a corker, had lots of starch in her one time. She must be close to a hundred now but I remember she was awful sick thirty-five years ago. Lost all kinds of weight. No bigger than a wrinkle on a bed. Her son Gerald and his wife figured she was finished, and tell you the truth they couldn't wait, since they thought she had some money from her father. But anyway this Gerald and his wife—what's her name, Irene I think it was—didn't they go out and pick out a new dress for Lena's wake. Didn't mean anything by it, they claimed. Just wanted to be ready in case of the worst.

"Well, didn't Lena bounce back up like a bad cheque. Better than ever she was. And didn't she hear about the dress. She went around telling everyone she met: 'Did you see the ugly dress that pair picked out for me? What a sight! What were they thinking of when they bought that?'

"Dan Walsh himself egged Lena on, just to be bad: 'Maybe it was on sale Mom,' he goes.

"'Maybe it was,' she says. 'It'd be just like those cheap buzzards to do something like that. Make me look ridiculous at my own wake. I'll pick out my own dresses—thank you very much.'"

"That's the scary part," said Stan, who also knew the story. "They're both gone, Gerald and Irene, and there's Lena still on the go. More or less. She never bought them any going-away outfits that I know of, either."

"Nice of you to bring over a few things, Ree," Wally said, before starting in on the perogies. He blessed himself as he spoke, so that it wasn't quite clear whether his prayer was directed to Ree or the Almighty.

Lots of people thanked Ree and Stan. When they arrived at their camping site up in Inverness County, the first thing they did was invite their fellow campers over for a shot of rum and some cabbage rolls or whatever they happened to have in the trunk. When they went to the Legion for their weekly dart game, they brought along enough cold cuts and fresh biscuits to keep up their team's morale through the evening. No one was surprised any more. It worked well for Stan too because it gave him a chance to grab a bite without attracting much attention to himself.

Stan and Ree left Wally's once the perogies and the brownies were finished. When they arrived home Stan carried four bags of groceries into the kitchen. He could smell a trace of Ree's shepherd's pie still hanging in the air. The scent was slight and he only picked it up because he knew that's what they'd had for supper.

Few people would have noticed any odor at all but their son Winston's girlfriend Michele was one of them. She was thirty years old and had been a practicing vegan of some description since she was nineteen. Michele was quite thin. She claimed to have a highly developed sense of smell—"my olfactory sense," she called it—especially around food. Winston and Michele worked at the same call centre, but on different shifts.

STAN NEVER FORGOT MICHELE'S FIRST VISIT to their home in Groves Point last Thanksgiving.

"Come in, come in. Happy Thanksgiving," Ree greeted Michele at the front door with a warm hug.

"Winston was called out to work at the last minute; he'll try and get over later on," Michele explained. "That's what it's like when you're assistant supervisor."

"Oh, too bad," Ree said. "But it's sure great to see you. Our turkey's almost done. It's a butterball."

"I never eat turkey," Michele informed them. Stan noticed that in her hand she carried two small plastic trays with blue covers, one in each hand.

"Oh, that's too bad, but there's lots of other stuff," Ree replied, heading towards the freezer. "Let's see what we've got going here today," she said, as she opened the freezer door. "I see baby back ribs, sirloin steak, lamb chops for a start. Even got some of our Gagetown spaghetti and meatballs. They're not bad are they, Dad?" she asked, turning towards Stan, who sat in the kitchen.

"It's all good eatin', dear. Just depends what Michele feels like."

"How about some venison? We've got lots of deer steaks left.

Won't take a sec' to heat something up. What about some rabbit pie?" Ree continued with her full court press.

But their slim young guest steadfastly held her ground.

"Actually I've brought my own lunch. See." Michele held up her trays.

Stan and Ree watched as she lifted the blue covers. One contained some damp brown rice, while in the second was a copper-colored substance which Stan couldn't identify. Later on Winston told him it was likely a variety of local seaweed Michele favored.

"Actually, I'm a bit hungry right now."

And with that, even though the turkey had not yet been carved, Michele began nibbling at her meager rations. As she ate she stared dubiously at Stan's smart new leather vest and his old black leather ball cap with its Chevy decal.

Between mouthfuls, she put her cards on the table, making Stan and Ree aware of her deeply held, long-standing views on food and eating. How she avoided all forms of meat and animal products or their derivatives. That Winston was becoming sympathetic towards her views as he seldom ate red meat anymore. Although she did hear by the grapevine that he still frequented the local Kentucky Fried Chicken outlet when she wasn't around.

Ree stood in the middle of the kitchen. She was as still and silent as Lot's wife, as if she too had seen some forbidden sight. Stan, like an experienced general in the heat of battle, was quick to grip the situation. And on that beautiful October afternoon, Stan Webster knew as clearly as he ever knew anything, that he had witnessed a turning point in his family.

Ree and Michele would never hit it off.

Oh yes, they'd smile politely at each other. They might even accompany each other to some neighbour's wake. They would speak on the phone when necessary. But for Ree, Henrietta, his treasured partner and little house ruler, even if she lived to be a hundred like old Lena Snow, nothing—not the passing of time, not the advent of grandchildren or the unimaginable—nothing would ever really undo the impact of this first encounter.

Later, Stan replayed the situation many times in his head. Perhaps if Winston hadn't been called out to work at the last minute that Thanksgiving Day, he might have managed to smooth things over. Would things have then turned out differently? Dear knows. Maybe if Michele had been able to bend her principles ever so slightly. What if she had accepted even a single turkey wing as a token gesture? Could some flicker of genuine warmth have arisen between them?

But Ree's deep disappointment and Michele's cool indifference to this were so raw, so to speak, that an invisible chasm had split open between his wife and his son's future wife. Stan knew that an unbreakable pattern had been set.

He thought of his blue beret carefully tucked in the bottom drawer upstairs and the many conflicts he had faced while wearing it. But he realized that even with all his peacekeeping skills acquired in the tension and strife of Cyprus and the Golan Heights—he could never change things between Ree and Michele. He would just have to make the best of it.

Stan moved his head slowly from right to left, but he no longer detected any trace of the shepherd's pie in the house. Ree had taken off her lucky brown sweater and was busy putting away the groceries. He checked the thermometer outside the window of the back porch. The temperature was mild. No rain was forecast.

"Goin' after a few night crawlers, hon," Stan called.

He picked up his flashlight and his worm bucket and with a determined air, Stan ventured out into the darkness.

*H*ardscrabble

PAUL MACDOUGALL

*K*INNON WAS HOLDING ON TO DUKE with both hands while Peck was tying the second muff onto Prince's strong legs. Peck caressed the leg as if it was the first time, like when he was a young man and first touched his wife's leg. He took care to gently pull the muff up around Prince's spur and then tighten it in place. It went up smoothly, like the garter he slipped up Rose's leg some fifteen years ago. Now with both Duke's and Prince's spurs protected by leather, it was time to let them spar awhile. The birds would go at it against each other but would suffer no serious harm as long as their spurs were covered. If left unguarded, though, a spur could tear a gash in an opponent just as easily as a well-driven punch could cut open a boxer's face. And in Cape Breton in the 1920s they'd all seen plenty of that.

At fourteen Kinnon was used to handling the birds and Duke was no different from any other fighting cock. If you spend time with them, treat them right and feed them properly, you could pick up a rooster like a cat. This one was his favourite. His father promised him he'd eventually give him full ownership of Duke if he'd help him train Prince for the biggest fight of his life. Like eye or hair colour, Kinnon seemed to have inherited his father's love of fighting birds. Duke would eventually become his own Prince.

"Are we ready, Dad?" Kinnon said when he saw that Peck had both of Prince's spurs safely tucked within their muffs.

"Yeah we are, boy. Why don't you step into the ring first? Then I'll take Prince in."

The ring was built further back of the house in a clearing behind some trees. Though the cops wouldn't bother them, considering a lot of police were cockfighters themselves, there was no need to make things obvious, especially when gambling was involved. Peck's pit was built years ago with the help of his Uncle Danny and was ideal for training birds. The walls were made of old lumber and two-by-fours scrounged from the coal mine, and had stood the test of time due to the thick layer of creosote Danny had coated them with before pounding various sections into the ground. Danny had long since given up raising birds of his own but would always show up when Peck had a bird in the mix at a neighbourhood match. What with his black eye patch and numerous scars along his face, Uncle Danny looked like he had tangled with the devil, and his appearance at his nephew's fights often lent a sense of historical rooster irony to the afternoon battles.

The boy climbed over the wall of the cockpit, holding his bird like a leprechaun with a pot of gold. Kinnon was interested in the birds and didn't want to disappoint his father. He was more like his mother than his younger brother Alec, but he knew if he wanted any of his dad's attention he needed to stick with the birds. When Peck offered him a chance at being his helper at the upcoming fight in New Waterford against Jim Petrie's gamey bird, he jumped at the chance. They'd been sparring Prince with Duke for a few weeks now and Kinnon knew he had to do everything right, otherwise his father would get upset. He'd recognized in the last few days that Peck was more anxious than ever about the fight and had assumed it was because this fight was against such a champion adversary, The General—as Petrie so named his bird.

Duke was scrambling a bit when he got into the ring in anticipation of what was to come next. Fighting birds that took an instant dislike to each other would carry this to their grave. If you started two birds fighting when they were young, they'd kill each other as early as three weeks old. Peck had once described to Kinnon how, as a young fellow, he saw two little chickens beat away at each other till their eyes closed over. "They were literally beating themselves blind," he had said. "Then Pa took them out of the ring and put them into separate pens. They healed up good over a week or so. He fed them well and let them both rest. Then he took a bunch of other birds and tossed them in the ring. So he gets the two fighting ones and puts them back in the pit with the crowd of other birds. All roughly the same age, size and weight."

"And what happened?" Kinnon had asked his dad.

"Well, the game birds ran by all the others without even a glance at them and started to pick up the fight where they left off the week before. Pa let them go at 'er for a few minutes, then took 'em out and separated them off again. He did the same thing two weeks later. Guess what? They squared off again. You see, they remember their first enemy and won't be satisfied till he's dead. It's bred into them. Fight the other fighter till he's dead."

"Seems savage, Dad," Kinnon remembered saying.

"It is, boy. You ain't going soft on me, are you?" he remembered his father answering back.

DUKE NEAR FLEW out of Kinnon's hands when Peck entered the ring. He was carrying Duke's mighty adversary, the Prince of Glace Bay. Peck had debated long and hard which of the two birds was the best in the ring and had settled on Prince a while back. This made Duke his sparring partner. If Kinnon worked Duke well enough he'd get his chance to fight as well. But for now it was just a few short muffed-up sparring matches that he'd have to settle for. Like a prizefighter that was always waiting for a chance at a title belt, Duke would have to wait his turn too. Prince was by far the better bird, but Peck was sure these matches with Duke would keep Prince tuned up like a well-coiled spring. Ready to be unleashed in his full fury in a few days time upon that chicken from New Waterford, The General.

"You let him loose first," Peck said to his son. "Just lower him to the ground, then let him go. No sense getting caught up in the middle of two angry roosters, is there?"

Kinnon did as his father said, then scrambled over the top of the cockpit. Peck released Prince within a second of his son clearing the cockpit wall. He jumped over next. The birds flew into each other like a pair of banshees.

Prince hit Duke with a series of quick strikes. Though covered with a thick leather muff to prevent injury to the sparring bird, and also to avoid injuring a natural spur, the fighting cocks still went at it with both legs slashing. Their fighting instinct to take out another male was to attack with their legs and hope their spurs would disable the other bird. Peck estimated that Prince could strike up to twenty-five times per second. His father had told him, "It may look like it's only a few times, but them birds can strike like lightning."

Once a game bird was into a full-fledged attack, it was a ferocious sight to witness. Peck could see from the blur of legs before him that his old man was right. Speed was of the essence. If Prince had been unmuffed and outfitted with his own set of fighting spurs, Duke would probably be finished by now. Running the training oval upwards of twenty times a day had given Prince an almost unbirdlike strength. Duke was a good bird but couldn't match the speed and accuracy of Prince's well-placed kicks.

"Jesus, Dad! He's gonna kill him, spurs or not!" yelled Kinnon. Duke was trying to back away from Prince enough to give him some form of a run at his opponent, but Prince was having none of it. He was bearing down on Duke at an unmerciful pace. Unlike the strange and unique quality of Cape Breton boxers, who are usually friends with their sparring partners and don't want to really hurt them, a fighting bird will kill his sparring mate if he has a chance. To the bird another male cock is a direct threat to his barnyard rule. The hens are all his to take and plunder, and every other male bird worth his weight in grain is an enemy.

Peck usually let them go at it for about ten minutes, but he sensed an increased aggressiveness in Prince plus an urgency in Kinnon's voice. It was the boy's first bird and Peck knew Kinnon would be upset if Duke were seriously injured. But Peck thought with the big fight a few days away, a taste of chicken might be just what Prince needed to put him over the top.

"We'll let 'er go at it a couple more minutes," said Peck. Duke was up against the side of the cockpit now. Prince was slashing and slashing away. The whack of the muffs was almost as loud as the squawking. Both birds were in a state of frenzy. Prince in anticipation of the kill, Duke fearing the same.

"Dad!"

"One more minute! You ain't going soft on me now, are you, boy?"

"No, Dad! He'll kill him!" Duke was down. "Jesus, Dad," Kinnon said as he jumped over the wall of the ring. He stuck his gloved arm between the two birds.

"Christ almighty," Peck shouted as his son tried to separate the two birds. He jumped in after him and grabbed Duke by the neck. "For God's sake, boy, you'll get yourself cut to pieces by the beaks!"

Prince flew up like a Halloween witch. The bird was enraged. Peck had to duck as Prince dove headfirst for Duke's exposed breast. He was being robbed of his victory.

"Get out, boy! You ain't ready for this, I guess!"

Peck threw Duke outside the ring. Prince threw himself at the wall. Kinnon jumped out after his bird. Peck was right behind him. The boy was chasing his bird into the woods. Peck looked at his prizefighting cock still screaming and tearing around the ring.

"At least you're ready," he muttered to the bird as he wiped the blood and dirt from the cockpit off his hardscrabbled face.

What Angel Wakes Me

RUSSELL COLMAN

*M*EN AND WOMEN MINGLE in the gallery behind me. I hear muffled speech and muffled footfalls as they move across the polished floor. I'm alone at the end wall, standing before a picture of Bottom the Weaver, a simple man cursed by a cruel joke to wear an ass's head. He lies on a bed of flowers in the nuptial bower of the Queen of the Fairies. The painting illustrates the moment in Shakespeare's *A Midsummer Night's Dream* when Titania, the queen, first sees Bottom. My grandfather painted the picture.

I'm deep in the memory of the night when, as a nine-year-old boy, I snuck out of the house.

Four people approach quietly from one side and interrupt my reverie. They praise my grandfather and his work. They offer their condolences; he died three months ago. Twenty-five of his paintings and drawings, a retrospective, are mounted around the gallery. On a table in the center of the room, an urn, flanked by a single candle and a bowl of roses, holds his ashes. This exhibition is his memorial service.

My grandfather was, for most of his adult life, an illustrator. Successful from the beginning, by mid-career his originals were sold and collected as artworks in their own right. Early on, he worked in oil, then acrylic. When he retired, he returned to pencil and charcoal. Unburdened by narrative reference, his selection of subject matter seemed almost random, simple scenes of nature, scenes that might easily go unnoticed. He drew with a freer hand, more relaxed, more spontaneous, yet with piercing detail. Later, in his final years, he took to adding with his finger a single smear of raw colour to each picture—a streak of blue that drew the viewer in and said "see how blue this bench is"—a single daub of saturated red saying "look more closely at this glint of light on the wheelbarrow."

The four people—a literary agent and his wife, and an author of children's stories and his partner, a man who is himself an illustrator—turn to the picture.

The woman reads the brass plaque on the frame, "*What Angel Wakes Me,*" she says. "Enchanting."

Her husband says, "From a limited edition of *A Midsummer Night's Dream* printed to celebrate a publisher's wedding. A very rich publisher."

The five of us stand at the painting in silence. Then, after assuring me of their sympathy and sharing polite goodbyes, they move off. I'm alone again with my grandfather's painting, seeing Bottom as Titania sees him, not a beast to be mocked, but a man transformed by the sublime ardour of a fairy queen. In the picture, Bottom is no buffoon. He's real, a luscious creature with hair like sable, eyes like brown opals, lustrous under heavy lids. His teeth glisten; his lips bid you closer. Who would not desire him? the picture asks.

Looking into Bottom's eyes, I see or imagine I see the reflection of the fairy queen, and she returns me to my childhood memory of a secret expedition into the night. The transit from my room to the kitchen was as stealthy as my imagination could make it. Holding my breath, I tiptoed down the stairs and crept with slow, exaggerated steps to the back door. Listening for noises from upstairs, I felt, more than heard, the click of the doorknob in my hand. A glance over my shoulder and I'm out on the porch.

The silver birch trees, now truly silver in the moonlight, guide me down the lawn to the shimmering surface of the lake. The dock puzzles me because memory tells me the dock is gray, but now it's lustrous blue and the little red rowboat tied up beside it looks almost black.

The wet grass tickles my ankles. Dad mowed the lawn between the house and water our first day at the cottage. He does this every year. And every year his father—my grandfather—tells him it would look better left alone, but it always gets cut. "Stubborn," says Grandpa. "Like father, like son," Dad replies. But it's Mom who prompts the mowing ritual. This ritual comforts her, even though, inevitably, the grass grows long again, softening the edges of the lawn and now tickling my damp ankles.

The morning before my big caper, I went down to the lake with Grandpa, going slowly because he uses a walker. He doesn't like it. Sometimes he pretends to forget, but Mom, each time, insists. "Best to do as your mother says," he tells me. When we get to the place where the lawn flattens out, we rest under the birch trees. There I see a sparkling grass-spider web—something new, something until now unnoticed. I drop onto my belly, my face close to the grass where the web hangs like a translucent canopy. Drawing back and raising my head just a bit, I see more of these webs around me, some big as dinner plates, some no bigger than the palm of my hand, and all sprinkled with tiny mirror-balls of dew.

"Look at these, Grandpa."

"It's the fairies."

"Fairies?"

"Yep, they were here last night, holding their revels." Grandpa shifts his weight to the walker, lowers himself to his knees, and shoves the walker aside. Then he answers the question he's planted in my head.

"It's a big party with music and dancing. Maybe even costumes."

"And the fairies have revels?"

"They do. At night, their king and queen meet by moonlight with the noble men and women of the court, their servants, and soldiers. They camp among these canopies."

His gesture takes in a group of webs. I stand to take in the size and shape of the camp.

"See the big one in the middle?" Grandpa goes on. "That's probably where they have their party. Under that one farther off is maybe where they cook. Others are for sleeping."

An image of a soldier-fairy armed with a tiny fairy-weapon forms in my head.

"Maybe these little ones on the edges are for the guards?"

"Could be," Grandpa says. "And see there, off by itself, that's the fairy queen's bower."

"Bower?" Another new word.

"Her private place, set apart, where no one will disturb her or her king. Full of the most beautiful things. Carpets the colour of springtime crocus and autumn leaves. Cushions the colour of irises and roses. And everything can be packed up and moved."

"Like camping?"

"Yes, like camping." Grandpa smiles. I'm completely with him now. "Fairies move from place to place. They live everywhere and nowhere."

"So, the fairy queen has a sleeping bag?"

"More like a big hammock, with a mattress stuffed with the wool of cottonwood seeds and covered with flowers, like the coverlet on Grandma's bed."

I know the coverlet. And I remember Grandma. She died two years ago. Grandpa and I stay quiet for a while, remembering. He doesn't move at all. I sit back on my heels and brush my fingers through the grass. After several passes, I pull up an acorn cup.

I open my hand to show him. "Look, Grandpa."

He takes it and holds it close to his eyes. He examines it for what seems like a long time then says, "This looks to me like one of their wagons."

"Fairy wagons?"

"Yep. Wagons, with black beetles to pull them. But the wheels have broken off this one. Let's see if we can find them."

I get down on my hands and knees to look closer. Grandpa does too, but he needs the walker to get his hands down to the ground.

We're both down on hands and knees now, combing through the grass. I find a tiny twig. Grandpa says it might be the spoke of a wagon wheel. I collect our little bits of fairy debris.

Suddenly Mom shouts from the porch, "Oh God, Obie! Oh my God!" Obie is my name. She's calling me. At the sound of her voice, I jump to my feet. She's still shouting "Oh, my God!" as she runs toward us.

Grandpa's up on his knees now looking at me, then straining to look back over his shoulder. He catches sight of Mom just as she flashes by and flings herself down in front of him.

"Dad, are you okay?" She's breathless.

"Yes, Beth, fine. Everything is fine."

"Did you fall? Are you hurt?"

"I didn't fall and I'm not hurt."

She helps him up and into the walker saying, "You scared me to death!"

"Sorry to frighten you. Just out here exploring with Obie."

"Let's get you up to the house and fix you some iced tea. Or maybe lemonade?"

"Tea's fine, Beth."

"Want some lemonade, Obie?"

"No, thanks, Mom. I want to look around some more."

I stay down by the lake until lunchtime gathering up whatever looks to me like archeological remains of a fairy revel. After lunch, I show them to Grandpa. Together we assemble the artifacts and speculate about the uses and meaning of these treasures: a curved piece of bark could have been a boat, suggesting to Grandpa that the king may have crossed the lake on a royal barge; a feather no larger than my little fingernail might have fanned the fairy queen.

That night at bedtime, I decide to see the fairy revels for myself. I lie awake until just after midnight, that being the latest I have ever been awake, then sneak out of the house.

Now with chilly feet in wet grass, I look for a place to wait and watch. I find a dry spot beneath the bushes near the place that I explored so closely earlier in the day, and sit to begin my observations.

I worry that any noise might frighten the fairies so I stay still and quiet. I listen for any sound, thinking I may hear them before I see them. I make a list in my head of what I hear—the splash of a fish; the plop of a frog leaping into the water, this I heard twice; and the cry of a loon, but that came much later. I don't hear the fox approach, but I see him. Watching him pad across the lawn, I imagine the sound of each individual leaf of grass bending under each paw as it comes to rest.

I'm so quiet I feel like I'm not even breathing, like I'm not here at all. But the fox knows I'm here, and never takes his eyes off me until he stops very close, just beyond my reach. He looks right, then left, then sits. The fox stares at me and I stare back. When he nudges up his nose to sniff the night air, I hear the sniff. I watch him watching me until he stands and moves toward the lake. He veers around me and dashes to the bushes, but just before he disappears, he stops and turns to look at me once more. He's inviting me to follow him, I think.

"I'm sorry I can't go with you," I say aloud. "I'm staying here."

The fox seems to wait politely for me to finish my apology, then leaps into the bushes and is gone. The moon is high and brilliant in the cloudless sky. Never before have I known this magical blue light so intimately.

I pull my bathrobe around me and gather the collar up close

to my neck. Lying on the ground so I can peer beneath the canopies, I wiggle into a comfortable position, and watch.

Fireflies come first. Flashing gentle green lights all the way up to the cottage and out over the lake. The fairies come later. One, then another and another, like the fireflies. Wings flash in the light of the torches they carry down to the canopies. I watch for a long, long time and see everything Grandpa talked about and more. When the king and queen dance, I see the queen looks like Grandma.

I hear the fairies too, just barely, and add their music to my catalogue of night sounds. As the king and queen make their way to their bower, the fairies play a lullaby with little bells, tapping and humming, and the faint whistle of a tiny flute. The last sound I hear that night is a loon calling across the lake.

In the morning, the spider webs are silent and pale in the dawn light. The fairies are gone.

Mom thwarts my plan to sneak back into the house when she meets me at the door. She doesn't expect to see me there and this delays her reaction.

"For heaven's sake, Obie, when did you come down—" She stops and looks me over, head to toes. "Your robe is damp. Your feet are wet. Have you been outside?" No answer. "All night?"

I don't respond. I want to see Grandpa.

Mom feels my forehead with the back of her hand to check if I'm sick. "You're okay," she says, kissing the end of my nose. "Go upstairs and put on something dry."

Later, in the kitchen, dry and dressed, I eat my cereal. Mom's not saying much. Dad's reading the newspaper.

"Obie," Mom says, "what were you doing outside last night?"

"Watching the fairy revels."

Dad winks at me over the top of the paper. It's a message, but what does it mean? Has he seen them too?

"You're not supposed to be outside at night," Mom says.

I look to Dad for help, but he doesn't see me.

Mom goes on about dangers in the night and appropriate times for appropriate activities. I'm not listening. I'm eating my cereal. I want to talk to Grandpa.

When I'm finally alone with him, he says, "Trouble with your mom this morning?"

I tell Grandpa everything about staying up and sneaking out, waiting and watching, what I heard and what I saw. I even tell Grandpa about talking to the fox, a detail I share with my mother only years later, when we would laugh about it, but that morning, I knew that including a wild animal in my story would only make the situation worse. My voice cracks when I tell him Mom didn't seem interested in fairies at all.

"Perhaps your mom's never seen them. That would make a big difference."

"Well, I saw what I saw, Grandpa, and I know what I know!" I'm trembling and my eyes sting. I'm angry and I don't want to cry.

Grandpa turns to me from his drawing table. He takes my hands in his. I feel the gritty charcoal on his fingers and see his smile through my watery eyes. Leaning forward, he presses a kiss to my forehead.

"Of course, you do, Obie." His face is close to mine, close enough for me to feel his breath, as if he's speaking his words into my eyes.

*L*and *W*ar

STEWART DONOVAN

*I*N AUGUST OF 1945 our father's thoughts were far from the war: he was checking his uncle's salmon net beneath the sharp rocks of Middle Head, not far from Corson's old home which the provincial tourist board had just recently christened the Keltic Lodge. As he pulled the cool, wet twine hand over hand, his heart quickened slightly when the starburst of writhing silver—two and three feet long and weighing as much as thirty pounds—came into view. And as he freed their gills and heads from the twine mesh he spoke to them softly in welcome until they slid over the gunwale into the flat bottom of the gently rocking dory. He had not eaten fresh salmon in almost four years and so he was anxious to row back to his half sister Nelly and have her boil the soft pink flesh in the traditional way with sliced onions, a few potatoes, salt, pepper, and some corn starch or flour to thicken the broth. As he rowed in the purple shadows and white whirlpools beneath the jagged cliffs—granite rocks his own Irish and Acadian ancestors had sailed and fished beneath for a century or more—he thought of the wealthy American, old Mrs. Corson, of his grandparents who were now dead, and of his own father who now spent most of his days in the back room of the old house that had been moved from the homestead on what was now Number Sixteen tee. That was twelve long years ago.

Despite his imagined or real hunger, Hugh did not row his

dory up the mouth of the Clyburn Brook to the traditional landing place, but hauled it up instead on the flat beach stones and eel grass close to what was now the Number Three green on the Highlands Links golf course—land that had belonged to his father just a few short years ago. He covered the slowly dying salmon with the tattered canvas sail to protect their soft flesh from the August heat, and then slowly walked towards the tee of Number Four green. Here a path that used to lead from their home on Sixteen tee entered the thick alders; the landscape that greeted Hugh's eyes was both remarkable and slightly foreign. The freshly mowed grass of the golf course gave off a sweet and pungent smell and looked remarkably like the undulating lawns and estates he had seen outside of London when he was on leave. Each tee of the course boasted a hand carved and varnished sign with Scots words carved in relief and painted black. The words on the signs described the nature of the hole for the tourist golfers: hole Number Four had been christened *Heich o' Fash*, which translated to "Heap of Trouble" because of its deep sand traps, wide water holes and elevated table top green.

Hugh heard the sound of laughter and the rattle of clubs, so he waited half-hidden beside a spruce tree on the left side of the fairway, until a threesome of golfers with their local caddies—he recognized one of the boys as young Simon McGean—made their way east toward Middle Head and another elevated green. Hole Sixteen was called *Sair Fecht*, which translated to "Hard Work" because of the mounds and hills you had to climb. When he reached the tee Hugh received a slight shock, as there was no sign that his family had ever lived there. He looked up the road which now led to Numbers Seventeen and Eighteen. The tee on Eighteen boasted a sign that read *Hame Noo*, which he believed was Scots for "Home Now." It was here that his grandparents Tom and Grace Young had lived, and he suddenly remembered the day he and his younger brother Hector had helped old Lewis Kassab get his wagon out of the mud, and how their reward had been a small ham to take home to their grandmother. Kassab, a Lebanese peddler, was taunted in public and private as an old Jew, until the day he finally left the village to go back to Beirut. There he found his bride and lived out the rest of his days in the village of his birth on the western slope of a mountain.

Hugh walked into the woods and stood by the old foundation of cement and stone. When he turned and looked towards the black and white spires of the church, he saw himself as a boy of seven, tears scalding his face, running in the direction of the Glebe House. Moments earlier, he had seen his mother Emma collapse on the floor and he had stood there in the heat of panic as his sister Veronica screamed at the flow of burgundy liquid that began to pool on the blue linoleum. When Hugh returned with Father Mickey, his mother was lying in the back bedroom in a coma, and later that evening, after the midwife had come, his mother had died.

"YOU WERE A LONG TIME getting those fish," said Nelly.

"I walked up to the old place to look around."

"I don't know what to make of that damn Park. There's lots of jobs goin'—look at your brothers Frank and Issy—but the way they treated poor Simon Hawley and Maryann Doucette—disgraceful, disgusting!"

"What happened?"

"You mean you don't know?"

"Nelly, in case you didn't notice, there's been a war on for the past few years."

"Don't be smart. You must know that Maryann and Simon were the last to hold out."

"Yes, I knew that."

"Well, let me tell you those government people can be savage. There's Maryann, a widow who's been teachin' school in this village for over twenty years, and she has to crawl under a barb wire fence to get to her home! They ran that fence all around her property and left her no right of way. Christ! When I think of it! Her husband John went to an early grave because his poor lungs were gone when he was gassed in the First War, and there's her two boys fightin' overseas with you!"

"Yes, but...."

"But nothin'! And there's poor old Simon Hawley never harmed a soul in his life—not like dozens of others I could mention—and what happens to him?"

"His...."

"I'll tell you what happens. Half his barn is knocked down by a bulldozer and his three cows and two horses run off into the woods. Oh, the sons o' bitches! And there's your poor father in there and I know what they gave him and your poor grandparents. That government is so mean it wouldn't give you a roasted fart. Just imagine what that old Mrs. Corson must have got with her lawyers and rich Yankee friends. It'd give you heartburn on your arse just thinkin' about it."

"She was a rich American—what do you expect?"

"Americans! And there's sweet little Teresa now thinkin' about marrying that sailor from Saskatchewan she met in Boston. She'd better bring him home first so I can get a gawk at him."

"Not much chance of that."

"No, I guess not. Any girl that has the nerve to leave home at fifteen for Boston can marry whoever she wants, I guess. The poor sweet little thing, I remember the day we put her on the *Aspy*, so tiny in that white dress she could have been makin' her Confirmation instead of headin' off to start a new life with your Aunt Flo. And now her latest letter says she's thinkin' about marriage. Well, as long as he's Catholic there won't be trouble. But didn't someone say that his last name sounded German—the Yanks won't like that."

Hugh started peeling potatoes while Nelly took the salmon that had been gutted and scaled and cut it into three pieces before placing it into a large cast-iron pot. She would parboil the potatoes first before adding them to the salmon so that the fish would not be overcooked. Moving about the kitchen in the familiar rhythms calmed Nelly down, and when she paused to look out the window at a passing truck she asked Hugh about his own future.

"Are you going to take that job driving truck on the park?"

"I guess."

"You don't seem too happy about it."

"It's a job."

OUR FATHER'S JOB WITH THE NATIONAL PARK did not last long. People who did not know him might assume that he quit work because, like his sister Nelly and brother Hector, he harboured a deep resentment against the government for evicting his family. But this was not the case. It was true that the war profoundly deepened his already natural contempt for government as it did for many young men of his generation, but it was equally true that it had altered forever his way of being in the world: To be alive and healthy and home was, for him, the equivalent of what his Catholic catechism had called a state of grace; it was, as he had often said, all that he had ever prayed for on his two-year journey through the hell and purgatory of northern Europe. He often remembered the half-finished letter he had taken from the pocket of the dead young man he had crouched beside on the beach at Normandy: it was written to the young man's girlfriend. Now that he had arrived back home in one piece and, as he so often said, in paradise—or at least what he considered its earthly equivalent—he was not going to tempt fate by complaining about things he could not change, about the world as it was. However, there were always things he could resist:

"I asked you to report here to Headquarters, Hugh, because your foreman says you were using a Park vehicle for non-governmental purposes."

"What do you mean?"

"Were you delivering groceries with the Park truck today?"

"I simply gave a crippled man from the village a lift to his home. He was trying to carry a twenty-pound bag of flour when I passed him on the road."

"Look, Hugh, I don't make the rules around here, but that kind of use of Park equipment is strictly forbidden. I'll let it pass this time but see that it doesn't happen again."

When he left the supervisor's office, Hugh knew that his days on the job would soon be coming to an end. His foreman Sanford MacLean did not like him or any other of the young veterans who worked under him. Isaac Doyle had warned his brother about MacLean.

"What's wrong with you, Hugh? Why don't you keep your mouth shut?"

"Issy, we weren't hired on here to use pick and shovel. We were hired as drivers. Anyway, he's just tryin' to get us fired because he doesn't like veterans. The old bastard's feet are as flat as Donald Duck's."

"Uncle Harry beat him up one time."

"How'd he do that?"

"Hit him with a rock."

Isaac looked at his brother and laughed.

"Here he comes back."

Hugh, Isaac, George Hardy, and several other young men were leaning against the side of the truck smoking when Sanford MacLean returned.

"How are things now, fellas?"

"SNAFU," said Hugh.

Isaac and Coady Doucette put their heads down and began to chuckle.

"What?"

"I just said everything is SNAFU and FUBAR. That's all."

"What, well, alright but are you going to finish digging those holes?"

"No, we're not. Are we, Issy? Coady?"

"Hugh's got a point, Mr. MacLean. We were hired to drive truck," said Coady, trying to suppress a wide grin.

"Jesus Christ, just because you young bucks spent some time hidin' in a goddamn foxhole in Holland doesn't make you any better than the rest of us. I'm gettin' pretty fed up with the lot of you. Noel, you and mister war hero here go down and pick up those men on Number Ten tee. Tell Peter we'll finish that shelter on the path between Twelve and Thirteen tomorrow."

When they got in the truck Noel asked Hugh, "What's SNAFU and FUBAR, anyway?"

"The Americans had those expressions. 'Situation normal, all fucked up'—which pretty much describes workin' for that old bastard. And 'Fucked up beyond all recognition.'"

"You get under his skin, Hugh."

"Yeah, I know, but I just can't help it. The guy's an idiot, Noel. Fellas like him didn't survive very long overseas. Either they shot him or we shot him."

"Do you think George will stay on?"

"I doubt it."

"He got shot up pretty bad over there, didn't he?"

"He was blinded for about a month. His tank got hit and his sergeant left him for dead. Joe Curtis from Bay St. Lawrence went back to get him, under heavy fire too. Pulled him out of the burning tank and dragged him back."

"Is that right?"

"Yeah, and Joe was never recognized for it either."

They were driving from the clubhouse along the newly tarred and chip-sealed road, and when they reached Number Two tee Hugh got Noel to take the short cut through Number Sixteen.

"This used to be your father's land, didn't it?"

"Yeah."

Noel pushed in the clutch and brought the truck to a stop for a moment: they looked out over the freshly cut green carpet that drew their eyes towards the white walls and black-crucifix-tipped spires of St. Peter's Parish Church, and then up and beyond the spires and their crosses to Ben Franey mountain and the surrounding highlands, purple in the distance.

"It's one of the best views around, Hugh."

"It's funny, I never realized what the place looked like till I got over there. Then I couldn't keep it out of my head, especially late at night, just before I went to sleep."

"How's your father doing?" Noel asked as he eased the truck into gear and slowly released the clutch.

"Not too good. He's still up and around."

As the truck rumbled past the church, the two men made the sign of the cross as they spoke, Noel faster than Hugh because he wanted to shift the Dodge into fourth gear.

"Father Mickey's goin' strong," said Noel.

"Yeah, well he won't be lonely anymore."

"Why's that?"

"He's got every priest from Halifax to Cheticamp wanting to visit him now."

"They're nuts about golf all right."

"Well, it's a poor Jesus substitute for a woman."

"You got that right. Did Hector ever tell you what he heard Father Mickey say to a couple of priests from Halifax?"

"No, I don't think so."

"You remember how Hector used to hide under the verandah when he was a kid to avoid being a slave for those nuns."

"Not just the nuns. Father Mickey made him work like a dog too. His favourite hiding place in the summer was up behind the steeples. We used to call him Quasimodo. Poor little bastard."

"The story?"

"Well anyway, these two young priests, who are keen golfers and just out of the seminary, ask Father Mickey what the people of Ingonish did before the golf course came. And Father Mickey says, rubbing his hand over his chin considering, 'Well, let me think, in the summertime they fished and they fucked. And in the wintertime they didn't fish.'"

Hugh laughed with his friend, trying to imagine the faces of the pious young curates. Religion ran deep in his family, as it did in all the families of the village. Mass had been said in his great-grandfather's kitchen for over forty years before a church had been built twenty yards away on land his grandfather had donated to the diocese. And last year, at the age of seventy-five, Hugh's own father had painted—for the fifth time—the seventy-foot-high steeples of the gothic structure he'd helped to build in 1913, when the old church had burned to the ground—an altar boy with a candle had fallen asleep at midnight mass. When Hugh met Hector in Sydney after his train journey from Halifax, his younger brother told him another story he had heard while hiding beneath the verandah of the Glebe House.

The year was 1934 and the government had all but finished its expropriations for the golf course, when two young bureaucrats from Halifax arrived to visit with Father Mickey:

"Would you like something stronger than that? I have some whisky or perhaps a shot of rum?"

"No, Reverend MacNeil, the tea is fine."

"Father Mickey, or simply Father, will do."

"Yes, well, Father we, as you know, represent the Province and the government is prepared to make a very generous offer for your land."

"What land?"

"The church land."

"Well, gentlemen, I'm not the one who has the say over whatever right of way or piece of land you'd want. That's the bishop's place and it might not even be his final say. But just out of curiosity, how much land do you need? I thought you had all you were going to take now."

"Well, you see, Reverend MacNeil, uh, Father Mickey, we want to bring the Fifteenth green down as far as we can...so that the hole will meet the specifications for a championship par five. And that means we'd end up in your graveyard and church."

"So what are you saying?"

"Well, we're willing to purchase the church and land. We would move the graves of course."

"And what would you do with the church?"

"Oh, we would have to knock it down, I'm afraid."

"But you would be able to build a much finer building with the compensation package," said the second civil servant.

Father Mickey, whose face had become even redder than it usually was from the drink, stood up, politely took the cups out of his guests' hands, and said, "Gentlemen, you have ten seconds to get off this verandah, into your car, and over Smokey—that's if you want to continue living in the state of health that you arrived in!"

As Hugh finished the story, Noel turned left at the Clyburn Brook and began to drive up the graveled road that gave access to the back eight holes of the golf course. It was here, two weeks later, that Hugh finally ended up quitting his job. Sanford MacLean had been harassing him whenever he got the chance, so when Hugh was crossing the brook with a load of gravel he deliberately stalled the truck mid stream. He waited until Sanford arrived and predictably began shouting that the kid from overseas couldn't drive a horse and cart let alone a goddamn three-quarter-ton truck.

Hugh turned the truck off for a minute, lit a cigarette, and calmly looked upstream at the setting sun. His foreman had been shouting all along, but now he suddenly stopped. The young veteran started up the truck, revved the engine and popped the clutch, buried the two rear wheels up to their axle in the quicksand gravel of the river. Hugh then jumped out of the vehicle and walked to the far bank of the brook to take the road home. He did not look back at Sanford MacLean whose curses echoed up and down the narrow and beautiful interval.

On the following Sunday, Hugh's father, John Doyle, had his third and final heart attack on his way home from nine o'clock mass. He had been sitting where he always sat in the second row from the back beside the pillar that divided the pew in half, and beneath the plaster cast station of the cross that depicted Jesus down on one knee for the second time. John's left arm felt numb, and the pain in his chest made it hard to breathe, so he asked young Emerson Barron to let him out. The congregation was lining up for communion, so he could slip out the back without anyone knowing; the choir was singing "Faith of Our Fathers" and he could hear the distinct strains of his son Frank's powerful voice above the others. Outside, the late September sun was warm and he took several deep draughts of air before setting out on the twenty-five-minute walk to home. Going down the small hill between Fourteen tee and hole Number Six he began to feel much better, so much so that he felt somewhat guilty about leaving church before communion was over. He even thought about turning around and going back, but decided against it.

When he reached the bend in the road near the Clyburn Brook a sharp pain almost doubled him in two, so he crossed the road and started down the path to his brother-in-law's house. He walked halfway down the narrow path and then sat down in the shade of a large Jack pine.

John Doyle knew he was dying, but he was calm, and as he lay back amid the soft pine needles and listened to the gentle murmur of the brook beside him, he drifted down the decades to when he'd launched his new boat the *Emma Marie*. Yes, he had named it for his young wife, and as he helped her aboard she had exclaimed how beautiful it was, how it had been worth every minute of work he'd put into it. Poor Emma, he thought, she had no idea what she was getting into, he should never have married her—she was too young—but that summer day they sailed to Ingonish Island with her holding the tiller while he set the sail. They watched pilot whales, called blackfish, nurse their young and point their noses to heaven off Middle Head as if they hadn't a care in the world. Then they dropped sail and sawed on hand lines until they both had brought a half dozen or more cod and haddock into the bottom of the boat—Emma shrieked and laughed every time she hooked one and John would reach over and help her bring the great fish over the gunwale. When they had all they needed, they sat back and ate the cold fish cakes, molasses sandwiches and raspberry pie that Emma had packed for the day. And after they had eaten John sat in the stern and Emma sat beside him, cradled in the crook of his arm. Her soft brown hair and sloping shoulders seemed to melt like mercury into the man who held her, as the child-like blackfish dissolved into the blue-purple sea beside them, and the boat slowly rocked in ancient rhythms of tide, currents and wind.

The Iceberg Galley

BILL CONALL

"*T*HE THING ABOUT THE ICE—"

That was how he began, though he pronounced it "oiyse." And left the "h" out of "thing."

"The t'ing about the oiyse is that people think it just lays there, but it's moving all the time, ice is. If it ain't floating away or banging into the shore, it's melting and getting smaller or freezing and spreading out. And you probably think there's only one kind of ice, but that's not right either. Now, you think about how many names there is for different kinds of rain, right? Mist, drizzle, downpour, sprinkle, shower, sun shower, driving, sleet and all that. It's the same with the ice."

I had asked what I thought was a simple question, completely unaware that I was speaking to the Cape Breton version of the Ancient Mariner. If I could have withdrawn it, I would have done so, but he was being polite in answering me so that required some courtesy. Also, he had me cornered.

"They call it the Iceberg Galley, but it wasn't an iceberg at all now, was it? People get that wrong all the time too. What it was was pack ice. Do you know what pack ice is, young fella?"

I said that I thought I knew, but I might not have spoken at all. He was away again before I got a third of the words out of my mouth.

"Now of course it all starts with it being cold, you see. If it ain't cold, no ice. Zero degrees is when fresh water freezes. Unless you're an American, then it's thirty-two degrees. It's all part of them people clinging to old temperatures, using a funny size gallon and miles instead of kilometres. You ain't American now, are you?"

I don't know if his question of my citizenship was rhetorical, but again he didn't rein in his conversational horse long enough to listen for an answer. The best thing seemed to be to smile and nod until he ran out of steam.

"In the first place, an iceberg is made of fresh water and it starts out as part of a glacier, you see? When a chunk breaks off and falls into the ocean, and they do that because the glacier is made of ice and the ice is always moving, right? So when a chunk breaks off and falls into the ocean, that's called calving. Like a cow dropping a baby, right? And then it floats around on the currents until it melts. They get a lot of icebergs down Newfie way, but they usually melt before they come this far. And they never come into St. Ann's Harbour anyway, now do they? They're too big and the harbour is too small, never mind squeezing through the narrows at Jersey Cove where the ferry crosses. Have you been on that ferry?"

I nodded, but it appeared that this time he was waiting for an answer. I said, "Yes."

"Well," he says, "can you even imagine one of those monstrous popsicles getting through that channel? I think not, sir! With the icebergs, the part that you see is only about one eighth of the whole thing, you see. All the rest is under water. So if you saw the top of a little bitty iceberg three or four feet above the water, then there's another seven times that underneath. And since the ferry cable lies at about twenty-five feet down, you'd be seeing pieces of cable all over the beach and the ferry drifting free. That'd be quite a sight now, wouldn't it? But it'll never happen."

"Is that because...?"

"And that's because we don't get icebergs in St. Ann's Harbour, remember?"

Of course I remembered, though it was becoming more difficult to keep track of the main point of the conversation. Conversation, hah! Diatribe would be more like it.

"But now pack ice, we get that all the time. It forms up against the shore north of here and there she sits the whole winter."

"Do you get pack ice here in the harbour?"

"No, no, we don't, and I'll tell you why."

This was not a surprise to me. He had latched onto me like a barnacle on a rusting hull and he wasn't about to let go until he was good and ready. That would happen when he ran out of stories, which was not a strong possibility, or when his bladder forced him to abandon the door frame and return to the urinal.

"It's the tides, of course. Out on the headland the tides are gentle, but you see how the bay gets more and more narrow at the ferry crossing? Well, the same tide passing through a much narrower opening just naturally goes a whole lot faster, too fast for the ice to form. I've seen the tide here run ten or twelve knots, and that's plenty quick, I tell you. The ice hasn't got a chance."

It being somewhat past the normal lunch hour, my family and I had been the only customers in the restaurant. After lunch was finished, I had been anxious to get back in the car and get going. The kids were acting their ages—five and eight—and they wanted to get outside and work off some energy, not be strapped in the back seat watching more trees and water and hills slide by outside the window. While I headed for a quick trip to the bathroom, Rita had taken them outside to run around and throw rocks into the harbour.

It would be a long time before any of them thought to come looking for me. I don't know where this old man came from, but I had been standing at the single urinal when he arrived. He had begun talking to me when he came in the door, continued while he released a long, strong stream into the bowl of the toilet in the cubicle. Was still talking when he came out as I was drying my hands on one of two real cloth towels hanging from the rack. In between shaking off and washing my hands, I had made the mistake of asking him about the name of the restaurant. He had bypassed the hand-washing stage and leaned himself against the only door at about the angle of an old pine tree that will be flat on the ground come next spring. Or the one after.

"This used to be called the Lobster Galley," he told me, "and that name worked well for a lot of years. Tourists, you know. Looking for their souvenir Cape Breton lobster dinner and willing to pay through the nose for it. But then there was the incident with the ice and those pictures must've been in every newspaper and on every television set in the world! Did you see the picture display out in the gift shop? I guess not, or you wouldn't be asking me about it, now would you?"

He was right about that. My wife had wanted to cruise the gift shop on the way in to lunch, but I had vetoed the idea. I was in a hurry, remember? The souvenirs could wait.

"So it was the kind of thing that might happen once in a million years, the combination of extreme tides and just the right ice. Or maybe longer. Everything had to be perfect, you see, or it couldn't have taken place at all. The winter was cold, this was four years ago now, with plenty of snow. Then it had warmed in March the way it sometimes does and then got extra cold again and stayed that way for a few more weeks. So between almost thawing and freezing up again, when the water refroze there was a seam along the edge of the original ice pack that was more brittle than usual. Now, ordinarily when it gets warm in the spring the pack ice sort of rots and weakens and small pieces break off with the tide. And some of that happened, of course, little normal-sized bits breaking off and some of them floating into the harbour here. But then things got different. Now, what do you know about tides?"

Tides! Oh God, if You're there, don't let him get started on tides!

"There's four a day, you see, two high and two low. But one high is higher than the other and one low is lower than the other. On the day of the ice event here, the highest of the high tides came in after the lower of the low had run out. Now you don't have to do a lot of thinking to figure out that in that situation there is going to be a whole whack of water changing places. Without that you never would have got the ice to behave the way it did and there wouldn't be them pictures in the gift shop and this place would still be called the Lobster Galley and we wouldn't be talking."

I placed the tide tables on the list of things I would curse when I had time. If I ever escaped from this bathroom, that is.

"Now when the low low tide pulled out of the harbour and into the ocean, the water dropped of course, and pieces of ice started to break off of the pack. But dropping the level so much more than usual put extra pressure on the ice, particularly on that brittle seam I told you about—d'you recall? Well now, it was still pack ice but it looked like an iceberg, it was that big. It would have been about a hundred and thirty metres long—do you know metres? A metre is about a yard and a bit—so a hundred and thirty metres long and about half that much in width. So if you're thinking in feet, that monster would've been about ninety-some thousand square feet on the surface and maybe a dozen feet thick. Now that's a chunk of ice! Not as big as an iceberg, but a respectable piece of ice all the same.

"And it started to move."

At the mention of moving, he shifted his position so that instead of leaning on the hinge side of the door he was favouring his port side and angled directly across the door handle, dashing any thought I might have had about making a break for it.

"Now I have no idea at all at all about what it might have weighed, but it would have been an impressive number. By the time the incoming water had gathered enough strength to make it move at all, the smaller bits of ice had already up and were long gone. It was like floating little chips of wood versus floating a whole log; it took a lot longer to get it in motion and up to speed, but once she was rolling it was going to take some doing to get her stopped again. As you will see, my boy."

If only I hadn't paid the bill before I left the table. The waitress might have come looking for me. Or the police. I would have welcomed either one. Hell, I would have welcomed a terrorist attack if it would get me out of the bathroom.

"Now she started moving broadside to the tide of course, but the further up the bay she come, the more the water started to boil up off the bottom and it turned her sideways, like lengthwise, if you know what I mean. Like a great big oversized log barrelling up St. Ann's Bay and headed straight at the ferry. Now you've seen the *Torquil MacLean*, have you not? She's not a big boat, and this ice floe was twenty times her size just on the surface alone, so if it came to a contest, it would be no contest at all.

"Joey MacDonald was driving the boat that day. He saw her coming, and if he could've hauled his boat up on the beach out of the way he'd have done it. But he couldn't, of course, so he did what he could do. He run her up on the Englishtown side of the channel, got everybody ashore, and then put all the slack he could into the cable to let it sink as far as it would. Then he went ashore himself, turned on the Out Of Service lights and stood by to watch what was going to happen.

"If the floe had been sideways to the tide, it would never have got through the gap and into the harbour. It would have wrecked on the shore on both sides and there would have been water a'boiling for a while, but no harm would've been done. But she was running lengthwise with the tide, like I told you, and she filled the channel from bank to bank on the way through. Now a normal tide can run ten or maybe fifteen knots, but this was an abnormal tide. Joey figured it was making close to twenty-five knots when that ice came through there like the Old '97 coming down the grade between Lynchburg and Danville. He said that the noise the ice made when it hit both sides of the shore at once was like there was going to be a hole opened up in the earth and they'd all wake up in China. It knocked the *Torquil MacLean* sideways and up onto the shore and busted the cable like it was a piece of string and not three inches of tempered steel."

In spite of myself, I was starting to find this captivating. He was a long-winded old coot, and he still had me trapped in the bathroom, but he was such a darn good storyteller that I was getting less and less concerned with getting out and more interested in the end of the tale. I uncrossed my arms and leaned back against the sink as he continued.

"So now this monster was impossibly through the gap and going lickety-split up the harbour under a full head of steam. Now you remember me telling you that the smaller pieces had gotten away quicker and were way ahead of the big one? Well, no more, for she had caught up with them and that was the final piece in the puzzle that was needed. As big a piece of ice as it was, if it had hit the rocks on the shore at the south end of the harbour, there would have been a mighty crash and chunks of ice buckled up here and there and that would have been that. For big as it was, rock is rock and ice is only ice and bound to break sooner or later. But that didn't happen, did it? No it didn't, and here's why.

"The top end of the harbour was chock full of smaller pieces of ice, nowhere near the scale of the monster, but good chunks of ice all the same. Now do you know about rafting?"

I allowed that I had never heard the term rafting used in connection with ice.

"Rafting is when a piece of ice going one way runs into a piece of ice either going the other way or going nowhere at all, and one piece slides up on top of the other one, you see, with the advantage going to the piece that's doing the most moving. In this case, that was the big one. When it started colliding with the smaller pieces, it pushed them right out of the way until they hit the shore and had nowhere else to go and then it started rolling over the top of them. Like I said, she was moving at a goodly clip still, and it was going to take more than a few ice cubes to bring her to a halt. So she kept on going and climbing over more and more smaller bits and driving them down to the bottom of the harbour like a ship coming into a dock too fast, until the smaller pieces had nowhere else to go and the lead edge of the big floe started to rise out of the water. Well, you can guess what happened next."

"She crossed the rocks and hit the building?"

"That's exactly right, my son. Climbed the rocks as quick as a squirrel over a log and the lead edge smashed through the plate glass windows all along the front of the dining room for about sixty feet and then came inside like a tourist barking that he was from the United States of America and he needed a window seat right now. Except that there were no more window seats by this time, nor windows either."

"Was anybody injured?"

"Nobody was injured, but there was one fella who didn't do what he should have done when everybody else did it, and he sure embarrassed himself. Edith MacLean was working that day and she could see the trouble coming, so she got everybody out of the dining room except this one man who was still sitting at his table and taking pictures of the ice coming. She yelled at him and tugged at him but he still wouldn't come, so she finally figured that if he's that big an idiot the world would be a better place without him and she took off to save herself. Well, he was still taking pictures when the ice hit the rocks with a tremendous roaring, and that was when it finally began to sink into his brain that there was some danger in the neighbourhood and it might be good to get out of the way. But he had left it too late. He just made it up the steps to the landing when the windows exploded and he made a dive for the exit. Caught his pants on the leg of a table and ripped the ass out of them at about the same time that his bladder let go and he soaked the front of those tan-coloured brushed-cotton beauties and turned them a dark brown before he scampered out the front door on his hands and knees. Without his camera."

"Good heavens! He must've felt about half an inch high."

"Maybe not even that. He got into a blue van with New Jersey plates and drove away. Didn't come back for his camera, didn't even wait for his wife! One of the other customers gave her a ride into Baddeck to their bed-and-breakfast, but neither her husband nor the van were anywhere in sight. I guess she must've found him or got home somehow, for she never came back either."

"Did some of the photos come from his camera?"

"Yes. The ones of the ice coming up the harbour. The other ones with what looks like a great huge ice cream sandwich sticking through the windows, those were somebody else's. Edith, I think."

"It's amazing that the whole building didn't get crushed."

"Yes it is, and it was just a matter again of perfect timing. There was just enough small ice pieces to lift the big one up so that the bottom of it caught the rocks just enough for it to come in the windows and then stop. If not for that, she'd've been lying full across the road for sure with a pile of broken sticks in her belly and no place to eat for fifteen miles in either direction."

"Well sir, that was quite a tale, and I thank you for telling me."

"You're quite welcome, young fella," he said, opening the door and holding it for me. "It's not everybody these days who'll take the time to listen to an old-timer like me run on. Most of them are in so much of a hurry to get somewhere that they go right past everything with their eyes on the road and when they get to where they're going, they haven't seen a half of what they could have."

I didn't have an answer for that so I just nodded and shook his hand. He asked me where we were bound.

"We were going to do the full Cabot Trail today," I told him, "but I think maybe we'll take a look at the map and spread it over a couple of days. Right now, I'm going to go join my kids and tell them what you just told me. And maybe throw a few rocks into the harbour."

Campaign

FRANK MACDONALD

MOST OF THE TIME everyone in this town gets along, but when an election year rolls around the tension starts to thicken. It doesn't matter what a legal document says about race, colour, creed or politics. The fact is that there are Liberals and there are Tories, and there is not a damned thing the law can do to make them tolerate each other in an election year. There's too much at stake for that kind of nonsense.

I learned my politics from my old man who learned it from his.

They were pretty good at it too, and the old man had a job every winter on the snowplow to prove it. Good party workers are rewarded in Cape Breton the way they are everywhere, but somehow it seems more important here. If you don't know how to teach or nurse then you better know how to vote. The mines were gone long before my memory started recording anything, so politics was the only career left around here. Sometimes it was the Liberals' turn to work and sometimes it was the Tories'.

The only rare political disease in the town was old Angus Taylor, a miner who worked out in Saskatchewan in the Thirties and got involved in unions, and remained a CCFer for the rest of his life, even after he came back to Shean where there has never been a CCF candidate. What he would do each election was poll an open vote. It's a political blasphemy to poll an open vote, and only a very angry Liberal or Tory upset with his party would poll an open vote right in front of the poll captains, always for the other party. It wasn't done very often and always for effect, and you could count that by the next election he would be back in the fold. Saved, if you were using religious examples. But not Angus Taylor. Every election he took his ballot from the poll captains and marked a big "X" across it right in front of them, spoiling it. When the CCF became the NDP he still called himself a CCFer. Stubborn.

The election when I was growing into my first vote was the one that made history in western Cape Breton. It never happened before and it hasn't happened since, but it caused quite a stir.

I got interested in the election simply because it was my first, the first time nineteen-year-olds could vote. The age of manhood had been lowered to include me, so I was taking a pretty good look at it. The telephone poles were patchwork quilts of red and blue posters covering each other because as sure as the Liberals would put up a poster the Tories would slap one of theirs on top of it, and the next day that one would be covered with another Liberal poster. Any bare wall in the town was the same. About the only time the party poster was unblemished was when it hung inside a store window. Even the store owners declared themselves, putting politics ahead of business. I don't know if it cost them money or made them money, but I do know that no Tory would go into a store displaying a Liberal sign, and vice versa. They'd quit smoking first. After the election, commerce returned to its usual patterns, but not during an election. If I went into Harry's Confectionery for something with the sign he had in his window, my whole family would be suspected "turncoats" or "fence-jumpers," and there wasn't a worse accusation a family could face in our part of Cape Breton, not even converting to another religion.

What made that election different was that after a couple of weeks, when the campaign was really gearing up, and the candidates were entertaining everybody with jokes about each other, Allan Rankin declared that he was going to run Independent.

The whole town froze in mid-motion at this news, and the other candidates behaved like a couple of dogs whose fun had been interrupted by a bucket of cold water. It wasn't as if some crackpot communist was running for the NDP. This was Allan Rankin, and he was running Independent. It was serious enough to make the front page of the Halifax paper, although the reporter remarked in his article that it wouldn't make much difference.

Allan Rankin was sour, that's what everyone knew. He had tried to win the nomination for his party a couple of times and lost, even though people thought he would do all right in Halifax. The rumour was, and it was never more than that, that during the war, in France, Allan Rankin disobeyed orders from his commanding officer. Rankin was a captain, and the other fellow was a colonel, and Rankin bucked him. The way some men tell it, Rankin was a coward, and the way other men tell it, a couple of them from our town who were there, he saved his men's lives because it was a dumb order that would have gotten them all killed. Anyway, the funny way politics works, the colonel became a cabinet minister, and his advice to the party was that Rankin couldn't be counted on to support the government, even if he was a member. Too independent, you see. So the way the people here looked at it, if they didn't want him in Halifax there wasn't much point sending him there.

The danger, the way the old man explained it to me, wasn't that Rankin would win. Christ himself couldn't run Independent in western Cape Breton and win. What the party was worried about, the old man said, was that Rankin might just pull enough votes away from our candidate to get the other party elected. Then where would we be? It made a lot of sense to me. So the first night Allan Rankin held a public meeting, I agreed to be a spy.

The parties always sent spies to the other party's public meetings to see what was being promised, and especially to see if there were any turncoats slipping over to the other side.

It was exciting stuff to be asked to take on a job like that, especially when the candidate himself does the asking. I was with the old man in campaign headquarters, the old man was handling the phones, and the candidate asked me if I would do him a favour. As if I could say no. But when I heard what it was I could only thank him. I thought he wanted me to run for coffee or slap up some posters.

The first thing I noticed was how few cars were parked in front of the Parish Hall. Inside there were barely a dozen people, and everybody sitting far away from everybody else. Of course, when I opened the door, they all turned around to see who was coming in, so I just sort of sat on one of the tin bingo chairs in the back of the hall. I knew everyone there, and they didn't matter much.

Allan Rankin was at the front of the hall talking to one of the men who had come to the meeting. He had his business suit on and it fit him like a magazine ad. He ran a pretty big business for a town the size of ours, and that was another thing people said about him, along with the army stuff, that he just wanted to line his own pockets in politics. He seemed to be lining them pretty well without politics, though. Finally, he looked at his watch, and then looked at the door like he was expecting more people to come. When they didn't, he walked up onto the stage and began to talk as if the place was full.

I went to political meetings with the old man when the campaign started and the hall, the same one, was packed. You could hardly see the stage for the cigarette smoke, and at the back the men—it was mostly all men—were milling around shaking each other's hands, passing the brown paper bag to each other, and cheering every time the candidate paused in his speech, especially if he fired off a good one about his opponent. It was exciting, even when you weren't exactly sure what was going on.

Except for Angus Taylor's pipe smoke and a few other cigarettes, the hall was clear when Allan Rankin began speaking to us. I couldn't quote you chapter and verse of what he said. I don't have that kind of a memory. But he went on about the way people in Cape Breton, especially in our part of Cape Breton, were hostages to the political parties in power. He had a better way of saying it than me, but the meat of it was that as long as there was no place to go to work, no mines or factories or mills here, then everybody had to depend on politics. Just about every job that comes along, Allan Rankin pointed out, depends on going to see the elected MLA. "You can't get work on your own." I remember those words. "You have to go ask someone in politics to get that job for you."

Of course, every time he said something like this Angus Taylor was grunting, "Right you are!" or "You got them pegged there, Rankin!" or something like that. Rankin said there was no difference between Cape Breton and Russia except that here politicians used jobs the way the communists used guns. He said he wasn't running independent to be different, but just to remind people that it isn't a foreign word. Everybody, he said, should be independent of politics.

I told the old man about it when I got home. He said Allan Rankin was just talking through his hat. "What do you think we'd have here if we sent Allan Rankin to Halifax?" he asked me. "Nothing, that's what. It's easy to talk that kind of gibberish when you're sitting pretty the way he is. The rest of us gotta look after ourselves. Tell him to go to Russia and make them independent."

I was flipping around in my bed that night like bacon in a frying pan. I couldn't stop thinking about the meeting long enough to fall asleep. What was really on my mind was Angus Taylor, even more than Allan Rankin. It was what he said to me going out of the hall. A couple of the people there went up to talk to Allan Rankin, but not me. Not Angus Taylor, either. I guess he sort of had his say all through Rankin's speech. But it was what he had to say to me that stuck in my mind. He said, "It's you young people need a man like that. Guts." He didn't know I wasn't really there.

The thought of it was the same kind of scary excitement you feel trying to take the River Hill at sixty miles an hour with the old man's car. I lay there making up stories about the way the election would turn out if I was working on Allan Rankin's side. I was the hero, of course, making the impossible happen. The idea of doing something different had a thrill to it. By morning I had decided.

What I decided made me sick. It was alright daydreaming about it, but as soon as I knew what I was going to do, I got sick to my stomach. It was thinking about the old man that did that. I just could never tell about him. Sometimes when it was like this he would just stand there and understand me, and maybe the next time he'd clock me right on the ear for whatever it was. I just never knew. So I didn't tell him. Not right away, anyway.

Allan Rankin remembered me from the meeting. I guess that was easy enough. Then he told me he needed all the help he could get, said it with a kind of a laugh that settled me right into the office he had opened in his own building. He had posters that had to go up, and all sorts of other things for me to do. One of the things I had to do was listen. He didn't say that, but it was easy to tell from the way he talked to you that he expected you to listen. Mostly it was about politics. His theories, you know. Like the business about Highland Scots.

According to Allan Rankin, Scottish people in Cape Breton were naturally loyal. It's part of our heritage, he said, to follow our leader. Our ancestors lived like that, loyal to the laird of the clan, trusting him to always decide what's best for the rest of us. After the Highlanders were driven out of Scotland, the lairds stayed behind. Sold out, he said. Our people landed in places like Cape Breton without the leaders they had been taught to trust. So they turned to new ones, clergy and politicians. But they never lost the trait of loyalty. Their political party was their clan now, the way their church was. What Allan Rankin said was that that loyalty was being manipulated by the Liberals and the Tories, who would never seriously work to make places like Cape Breton not need them anymore.

He had plans, too, and he talked about them like you were his business partner. "Look at that wharf," he'd say. "Why shouldn't there be a fish plant there?" Because it wouldn't work, I told him. Everybody in town, Liberal or Tory, knew that. "Why?" he asked me. I couldn't tell him exactly, but it was common knowledge. Then he tells me why it could, and I could almost see it there, looking down at the wharf when he talked. It was the same when he would talk about the woods that covered the mountains all around us, or a beach full of tourists.

The old man knew. He couldn't help it, considering the glee some people take in delivering bad news. For over a week he never said anything. We just never mentioned politics at the table, but it was hard to find anything else to talk about. What I suspected was the old man was as afraid to bring it up as I was. Without really saying anything, or even thinking that that's what I had done, I had declared my independence. It made us both awkward.

The thing that brought it to a head was my fault. Maybe because I was scared, maybe because I didn't want to upset the old man, I always took off my VOTE RANKIN pin and stuck it in my pocket when I was going in the house. I wasn't a cocky kid, and I knew the old man.

Then I just forgot. One day I walked into the living room with my jacket on and the old man looked up from the paper right at my chest. "There's a pin in that thing," he said, "so it should be easy to stick it up your arse."

"You wear yours all the time," I said, and he did, right on the front of his cap.

He threw down the paper and jumped up, taking a step

towards me. "Not in my house you won't! If you want to be a goddamned revolutionary bastard I can't stop you. You want to grow up into an old fool like Angus Taylor, criticizing, criticizing, criticizing, as if none of the rest of us had a mind of our own, then you go right ahead, but do it somewhere else. As long as you're under this roof you'll live by my rules."

I hung up my jacket in the hall, tucking in the side that the pin was on so it wouldn't show. I couldn't take it off, not then. I remembered to after that, though.

During the campaign Allan Rankin went knocking on every door in the constituency. Now the Tories or the Liberals couldn't do that. They knew what houses they could go to, places where the vote was certain, and the places where it was soft, the kind of a vote that could go either way. But they avoided each other's members like the plague. Allan Rankin didn't. He went to every door, sometimes with me driving him in his car, and everybody let him in. I thought that was a good sign, but he told me people were polite, and they were curious, but it didn't mean they were going to vote for him. "But if we can get a few to listen...," he said.

What he wasn't going to hold, he said, were any rallies. I figured that was because nobody came to the first one, but he said that they were circuses. "Roman Circuses" he called them. The Tories and Liberals held one or two a week in the constituency, and the way Allan Rankin put it, they were just to entertain the people. A couple of speeches that said nothing anyone would remember a day later, and then fiddlers and dancers and a big party afterwards, with the candidates going around shaking hands with everybody. He said it was a good way to distract people from the fact that nothing important was being talked about.

The rest of the time it was fun to be in the office. We weren't too busy, the few of us working there, since most of the phone calls were wrong numbers. Angus Taylor just about moved in, bag and baggage. He didn't do anything, but he knew an audience when he saw one. He told great stories about the Depression, when he was working out west, or trying to. He was fond of saying that this part of Cape Breton was the only place in Canada still stuck in the Depression. Then he would suck from his pipe, and blow out this big cloud of smoke, and say how the politicians liked it that way. Allan Rankin made that idea sound historical. Angus Taylor made it sound intentional.

Because everybody was so polite to Allan Rankin, we didn't really know how the election was going for him. The funny thing was, neither did the other parties. About a week before the election it started to show that they were worried about something. Both candidates stopped slinging mud at each other and turned the whole puddle on Allan Rankin; rumours about the war, about how he made his money, about our town being a laughingstock if an Independent was ever sent to Halifax from here. He loved it. Every time one of us told him something we heard, he laughed. "You can smell the sweat in those stories," he would say.

Just about that time, close to the end of the campaign, I was driving Allan Rankin someplace, turning out of the intersection at Main and Culloden, when my father's car turned up. The old man was driving his candidate somewhere, too, and we couldn't help seeing each other. He looked like I really embarrassed him. I could see him turning red, and feel myself doing the same. Ever since the fight about the pin we managed to avoid each other, especially outside the house. The sick stomach came back.

It was still there went I went home for supper. The old man was there, too. Waiting for the table to be set. I tried to stay out of his way. He was pacing like a caged animal. He wasn't talking to anyone, but I could feel whatever was on his mind like something thick and dark. I had enough sense to try not to disturb it.

He pushed his food around his plate, barely nibbling, and I knew it was coming, and the way it was building scared me. That was the way he nursed a rage, not letting it go until it exploded from him out of control. I just wanted it to stay in him long enough for me to get out of the house, but when I looked up to be excused from the table his eyes were riveted on me, and it was too late.

"I want a word with you," he said, the words coming out of him like he had strep throat. He pushed his plate aside and put his elbows on the table. Whatever it was, he wasn't mad at me. At something, but not at me. He was too nervous about the way he was trying to gear up to say what he wanted to say. He kept looking away from me whenever he went to speak, and especially when he told me that his candidate had had a word with him that afternoon.

"He told me I better have a talk with you," the old man says. He was purple. "He says he knows you're young. Wild oats and all that. But he said to me that he couldn't guarantee I'd get called back to the highway garage next winter. Too many men looking for those jobs who will raise hell with him if he hires me when they delivered their whole families to the party."

I never expected that, not to hear my father talking like he had a throat full of tears. He was scared as hell of me. I could see that, so scared that I jumped right in to tell him I'd go back tomorrow with him. I had to say it quick. I was afraid that if I didn't he'd beg me, so I never got to think about it until later.

The old man seemed to calm down after that. Then he dropped a softer shoe. He said that his candidate told him there was a good chance he could get me on at the highway garage in the summer, perhaps long enough to draw pogey for the winter. "Not many kids get a shot like that right out of high school," the old man said.

I guess I never got a lot of sleep that summer, because I was awake most of that night, too. I never thought of the old man when I turncoated over to Allan Rankin, betraying the family like that. But it made me feel like a rat having to jump the fence again, so I made an oath with myself that this was the last time.

It's one of the worst reputations you can get, and I wanted everybody to forget it.

The next morning I went with the old man up to the headquarters where he worked. People treated me like the prodigal son, and the candidate asked me a few questions about Allan Rankin and that was the end of it. Except that the candidate told me that I could be the party representative at our poll when election day came around. It was worth twenty bucks, he said, adding that a young fellow like me would have no trouble finding a use for that kind of money.

I made a point of not seeing Allan Rankin for the rest of the campaign, though. I don't think I could have stood it.

Election Day was like being inside a beehive. Representatives for both parties and for Allan Rankin sitting beside each other at the table passing out ballots to the voters. Drivers for all the candidates kept coming in and looking at the voting lists to see who had voted already, and who hadn't. If there was somebody they were pretty certain of, away they'd be to that house, knocking on the door, offering to drive anyone old enough to vote to the polls. Sometimes it was close to kidnapping, I think.

The old man was driving that day, so he was one of the first to vote. I passed him the ballot myself, and he took it and went behind the curtain. When he came out he was squeezing that ballot in both hands, like he was scared it was going to explode wide open right there in front of everybody, and was he ever happy to see it disappear into the ballot box.

I wasn't near as excited as he was when I went to cast my vote. I was looking at the names and I kept staring at Allan Rankin's. If I was sure it wouldn't make any difference, I probably would have voted for him. But I didn't. I had the old man's job to think about. And my own.

People who remember that election still talk about Angus Taylor's open vote. He walked into the poll puffing on his pipe, and asked for his ballot. When he got it, he opened it right there in front of us and took up a pencil. Then he leans right onto our table and begins marking his ballot. This time, though, he didn't scrawl a big ugly "X" over the paper, spoiling it. Instead, with everybody watching, he made his "X" as careful as a kid learning to write. Even his tongue was sticking out with the effort to do it perfect. Then he went over it and over it as though he wanted to vote for Allan Rankin a thousand times. When he put it in the ballot box he stood tall, breathing deep even with the pipe, and took a look at us. When he looked at me he gave his head just the tiniest shake. I looked down, studying my list until I felt him look away and start to walk out of the poll.

What happened that night was that our candidate got re-elected. But the really big talk was that Allan Rankin polled over a thousand votes. Nobody knew who, except for the fifty or sixty we knew for sure. When I heard the figure, I couldn't help thinking that he was probably happier than our candidate. Allan wouldn't even talk about five hundred votes when I knew him. There was more to the people he talked to than just being polite, I guess.

That election worked out well for me in the long run. The old man got his job the next winter, and I started at the highway garage that summer. When I did, the old man told me that if I played my cards right I could work it into a permanent deal, maybe even driving a snowplow. It turns out he was right. Except for one change of government, I haven't missed a winter at the highway garage in twenty-five years. But there's never an election comes around that I don't think about that first election... and wonder.

That's What Little Girls Are Made Of

D. C. TROICUK

*I*T BEGAN ON THE DAY OF CONCEPTION. Hers, not mine. Her tiny self was not yet eight hours old when already she was showing me who was queen of this castle. There I was bowing before the vanity sink in the light of dawn, blaming the unfathomable wave of nausea on last night's Anniversary Special at the Argyle Bar and Grill. Theirs, not ours.

Morning after morning in close encounters with porcelain and stainless steel I flushed one possibility after another down the drain—hangover, influenza, food poisoning. Then one of those mornings, in place of the monthly miseries, a germ of truth sprouted as bright and inconceivable as a crocus in winter snow.

It wasn't as if I was totally opposed to babies. One day I fully expected it would happen: I would tune in to the ticking clock and concede to husband, mothers and society at large. For now I put them off, pointing to convenient and distant milestones. When my career took off. When we had saved enough for a down payment on our dream house. And that vague catch-all: some day. Secretly I wished that if I was to give Charlie a baby, I could just *give* him a baby. Signed and sealed, diapered and delivered. Not by a doctor. By Canada Post.

On Charlie's bowling night I sneaked a much smaller package into the house and spent the longest two minutes of my life sitting there on the edge of the tub, awaiting my fate. Questions dripped into my thoughts like Chinese water torture, as if the results depended on advance decisions I had to make there and then. Would pregnancy have me racing out of project meetings or—worse!—bring me to my knees before the nearest waste-basket in the middle of a presentation? Would my career path be disrupted by weeks of maternity leave? Was I even ready for motherhood? How could I be, when I could mistake my own child for some gross bodily assault from within? I blinked away tears and focussed on the magic wand.

I hid the evidence inside an empty tampon box in the waste-basket, then retrieved it to check it. Twice. Three times. And still I didn't know whether I was happy or not. *Charlie,* I begged, *please come home.* My telepathic message went unacknowledged.

The radio tripped mysteriously off the ten o'clock news. Through the static and whine a distant oldies station crept in on the evening airwaves. I stalked around the house late into the night with Tom Jones stuck in my head. *Why, why, why, Delilah?*

When Charlie came to bed smelling of smoke and beer, I remained obstinately turned to the window, eyes closed, silently daring him to touch me. Wanting him to. All night I drifted in and out of Delilah dreams. By morning I understood: we were having a daughter.

When the alarm went off Charlie sprang from our bed straight to the shower. I lay there rubbing my perfectly flat abdomen thinking sorry thoughts. *Sorry—I didn't know you were in there. Sorry I tried to keep you from happening.* A more distant voice surfaced, the one that always popped up when truth was the last thing I wanted to hear. *Sorry I didn't want you.* I pushed the thought aside, prepared to make nice. "Hello, baby," I whispered. "This is your Mommy."

No response. Except from Charlie who called from the bath-room, "Who are you talking to?"

"Delilah," I said.

"Who?"

"Nobody." My response precipitated an immediate surge. I pushed him out of the way and fell to my knees in my morning ritual.

Rising to the mirror I looked myself in the eye, as if seeing deep into myself, to my womb. *So, little Delilah is a sensitive soul.* I blinked the thought away. But logic didn't keep me from rationalizing, from justifying my hasty word choice to someone who was not yet separate from myself, who was not yet anyone at all.

Delilah's roller coaster rounded a bend. The words sprang to my lips. "I'm sorry," I said.

Charlie cocked his head. "For what?"

I just smiled. The track had levelled off, the lurching car cruised to a gentle stop. Apology accepted.

For a week, in lieu of nighttime prayers, I bargained with my little passenger. "Just let me keep down one slice of toast in the morning and I promise—*I promise*—I'll tell Daddy all about you." But we were on mismatched schedules just now, me starting an intensive training course, Charlie on a tight deadline, one or the other of us going in early, working late. The delay did not sit well with Delilah. One morning as I wiped a cool washcloth across my pale face the eyes looking back from the mirror contained a message as if from an alternate personality.

"All right, *all right*," I whispered. "Today. I'll tell him today."

The queasiness abated.

A vaguely familiar sensation took over. Hunger. Ever since my little one had set off her internal rebellion, I had been avoiding the kitchen. The choices in our fridge—limited at the best of times—had narrowed drastically. The Domino's pizza box that had been there for a week. Clear plastic containers that showed greenish leftovers. Opaque Tupperware that hid the forensic remains of God only knew what.

I'd go in early, with Charlie, I decided. We'd stop at our favourite café for breakfast. We hadn't done that in a long time.

Delilah selected carefully from the menu. Our favourite waitress scowled her usual scowl and read my order back to me with an extra splash of sarcasm. "One poached egg, soft yolk, none of the runny white stuff. Whole wheat toast, light on the butter, dry if we've only got margarine. Orange juice, but only if it's fresh-squeezed. Or else the pulpy kind will be okay. Tea, but not out of the carafe. Make sure the water comes to a full boil, tea bag on the side. Milk, not cream. And while I'm at it," she improvised, "why don't I see if I can dig out that silver tray we've been saving in case Stephen and Laureen drop by."

I nodded. "That would be very nice. Thank you." I looked up to see both her and Charlie staring. "What?" I said.

I picked at my plate while Charlie scarfed down a stack of pancakes. "Is that all you're going to eat?" he said.

"I don't want to overdo it. I'm just starting to feel normal again after my...um...flu."

The fib generated a familiar pitch and roll below decks. I patted her under the table. *Patience, little one.*

"Charlie, honey...," I said.

The rough seas calmed. A knowing came over me. I had been laughing off the coincidences, ignoring the pattern, blaming it on my apprehension. But this feeling of unease had nothing to do with me. It was her. Delilah.

Panicked, I reached for Charlie's hand, searching for the words to tell him. But he was grabbing his paper, his kiss as sweet as maple syrup. "Later, hon. I'm going to be late."

My valiant attempt to break the news, though a failure, was rewarded. Delilah napped contentedly through the morning. As the instructor droned on, I surreptitiously checked my address book and encrypted my gynecologist's number into a mess of margin notes on the photocopied handouts. I would get to the bottom of this. I would prove this recent bout of foolish fantasizing about cloth diapers and breast feeding was nothing more than wild delusion borne of flu and fever after all. I mean, who *was* in control of my body anyway? I was. How could I not be? Our top drawer contained enough paraphernalia to put an entire city population on hold for a generation. The basic pen, calendar and thermometer. The intrusive combination Charlie referred to as "diagrams and condominiums." Discrete dispensers labelled for the memory challenged: "Monday, Tuesday, Wednesday...." All of these methods had been abandoned in favour of the latest thing—a home test that revealed fern designs in my saliva at a certain time of the month.

With sheer will power I guarded my true intentions from the spy within until break time. I cupped my hand around the mouthpiece of a pay phone in the lobby.

"I think I might be pregnant," I whispered, cringing as the doctor's receptionist broadcast my fears to the waiting patients.

"Preggers! Oh, Jenny! How wonderful!"

How easy it was to play to her enthusiasm. There in the lobby of the Westin Hotel I felt a glimmer of something like joy.

If Delilah sensed conspiracy, she kept it to herself. Or perhaps it pleased her that we would approach Daddy with nothing less than scientific results.

At noon I had errands to run and bills to pay, but Delilah awoke ravenous. She tugged me across the Rideau Street bus mall, through The Bay and out the rear door into the Byward Market. I could think of nothing but my home-town specialty: beaver tails—deep-fried pastry smothered in cinnamon sugar or raspberry jam or—my favourite—garlic-and-cheese. But Delilah's cravings ran contrary to my normal tastes. Up until now I was lucky to get my daily serving of vegetables from a lunchtime V-8, or a frozen pasta primavera in front of the early evening reruns. Today she slowed my feet beside stalls piled high with farm-fresh produce. We palmed the firm round bellies of watermelons and squash, fondled the cool texture of leafy greens, and marvelled at colours and scents I had never noticed before. We ventured into the Ontario Fruit Dealers and contemplated Ugli fruit and prickly pears and jicama, but came back to the stalls for local broccoli and carrots and what was to become our new snack food—snow peas—delectable, sweet and crunchy. They would never make it home. All afternoon I ate them out of the bag like potato chips.

We blinked in the sunshine while a rosy-cheeked lad in a giant fibreglass orange squeezed juice, one fruit at a time, into a gallon jug. At the Boko Bakery we passed up butter croissants in favour of seven-grain bread. The sight of animal flesh in Slipacoff's window made us turn away, yet the garbage-day stench of seaside refuse coming from the alley behind LaPointe's Fish Market drew us inside, our mouths watering for steamed mussels, poached salmon and Digby scallops wrapped, inexplicably, in spinach leaves. Was there time to get spinach? I shifted my load of packages to check my watch.

Delilah's eyes fell upon a single flat of brown eggs in the open door of a van. "I must have them," I told the egg man. Reserved for a regular customer, he replied. Personally, I admired his loyalty. But Delilah lit into him, working me like a ventriloquist's dummy. For all he knew we could be regular customers too. We could be better than the other regular customer, because at least we wouldn't keep him sitting here with his empty van waiting for us when he could be out there doing...chicken things. He stroked his chin, conceded that he did have things to do. When at last the eggs were ours, she moved my lips into a sweet smile. "See you next week," we said.

IN THE DAYS BEFORE MY APPOINTMENT Delilah settled into a contentment so blissful I began to doubt her existence. I thumbed through a travel magazine in the doctor's waiting room thinking ahead to next year's vacation—me, drinking coconut drinks served on the beach, wowing Charlie with the bikini I had seen in a store window....

A thought bobbed up like flotsam from out of a full-page azure blue pool. My Delilah was growing out of control inside me. Out of *my* control. My mind went to the basic arithmetic I'd learned in Miss Fanny Cohen's Grade One class. Two into two equals one. Two into four equals two.

Wait. That wasn't right. When two cells divide into two they equal...*four*. Four into two equals *EIGHT*.

My child was a mathematical genius! She was growing based on a whole different branch of mathematics. She was *multiplying* by *dividing*!

This concept of cellular super-intelligence feathered indiscriminately across every aspect of my life with Charlie, like a line of watercolour touched to wet paper. There was our chance meeting on a remote beach, a long-distance relationship everyone warned would lead to heartache. Then, just as we were about to call it quits, Charlie's sudden transfer and my fellowship had placed us simultaneously and unexpectedly in Ottawa, our mutual home town, at exactly the same time. At our wedding we had toasted the civil service and clerical errors. There was no other explanation.

Or was there?

I reconsidered our many misadventures in birth control. No sooner had the leftover wedding champagne gone flat than the adverse and inexplicable reactions had begun—to the Pill, to latex, to every spermicide known to man. I itched, I burned, I suffered a monthly bout of intense hormonal nausea not unlike the recent unsettled climate in my mid-section. Then there was the mysterious disappearance of both the thermometer *and* the calendar from my night stand. (We found them later in Charlie's toolbox in the garage. To this day he swears he doesn't know how they got there.)

Where was Delilah when all of this was going on? I pictured her, little Egg Delilah, lying dormant all through my youth, gauging prospects for Daddyhood from her Queen Bee throne in my ovary cluster. Orchestrating the near misses, the long days of waiting, the late periods that amounted to nothing more than that. Sending out her underlings each month, little kamikaze sisters who shot down the tubes to oblivion when—lucky for me—my boyfriends didn't measure up to her standards.

And then along came Charlie.

A less insightful person might believe wild coincidence had simply collided with reckless chance. I was beyond that now, flushed with the power of knowledge. Just yesterday I had smothered a plate of French fries in blue cheese dressing and devoured them with relish. If Delilah and her kind could make a person do that, they were capable of anything. Extrasensory communication. Telekinesis. So—clerical errors or forged signatures on transfer documents? Why not?

I rose unsteadily, needing to get the message out. I faced the row of women sitting there incubating their little despots in blissful ignorance. I opened my mouth to warn them: *They are in control! We are pawns in their tiny hands!*

Suddenly I was looking up at the tiled ceiling. Dr. Pelletier was hovering over me. Someone was holding my hand. "Lie still, Mrs. Nelson. You've had a little fainting spell."

DADDY WAS ON CLOUD NINE when he heard the news. No longer my secret, Delilah basked in his attention and patently ignored me. When she practised kick-boxing it was Charlie's touch that dispelled her nervous energy. When she was restless, it was his voice that lulled her to sleep. When he put his ear to my belly, he came away with ideas that could not possibly have been his own. He massaged my back and helped with the housework. And how else to explain why he would give up a weekend to take me to Toronto to a Leo Buscaglia lecture? The professor known as Dr. Love gazed out into the audience and addressed me directly. "If you have a fat belly, learn to love your fat belly." As if he had seen me that very morning posing side-on in the hotel mirror, trying to work up an appropriate admiration for Delilah's self-styled pink Cadillac formerly known as my body.

The moment soon passed when I believed this attention had anything to do with me. I was merely the vehicle. Part of me was jealous; another part said, *Shut up and enjoy it while it lasts*. Charlie had never been so attentive. The truth was, I was a happy Cadillac.

THESE ARE MY SLEEPY THOUGHTS as I rock my bundle into morning.

At home now, the congratulations pour in while Delilah practises in earnest what she has been training for all along. Manipulation.

I keep my theories to myself, but you cannot tell me she is not in control. She murmurs and I wake; she whimpers and I rise. I sleep, I eat, I bathe only when she allows it. I drop everything to tend to her royal needs. Guilt is like a bit in my mouth, bending me to her will. Guilt that I needed a C-section. Guilt that I can't breast feed. Guilt that is reinforced by the Grandmas who remind me, when she howls like Cujo, of my ill spent third trimester curled up with Stephen King.

Charlie smiles and cites male ignorance of such things. See, her Daddy has been wrapped around her tiny finger from the day he and I met. I wonder sometimes what would have happened if Charlie had not come along when he did. Would little Delilah have passed on the opportunity, let another lady-in-waiting take the call? Would she have made a kamikaze mission herself? If she had, would Delilah even *be* Delilah? I wonder. Because it wasn't until Charlie appeared in my life that she made herself known, fluttering her little Egg eyelashes his way, luring him away from the single life until he embraced the prospect of Daddyhood. I was the resistant one. Charlie—he was easy. Men are always easy. And women like Delilah are in control every step of the way.

Disposable Souls

PHONSE JESSOME

I JAMMED THE SHIFTER INTO PARK and knew it was murder before I killed the engine. One glance through the windshield told me that. Every cop has that vibe, that extra energy that comes with the big show. No one takes the oath to hand out parking tickets or lock up drunks. Catching killers, that's what the badge is really about. I stepped out to the rhythmic snap of yellow crime scene tape fighting an ocean breeze. Home.

I stood beside the car and pulled it all into my lungs, savouring it. The tape making all that racket strained away from me in a wide arc. The roof lights on two cruisers held it in place. They were nose deep in the ditches at either side of a gravel road. More tape stretched from the cruisers to nearby telephone poles. The road beyond the thin plastic barricade led to the blackened hills of the old city dump. I couldn't see the water beyond but I could taste the salt in the air. To the left, purgatory. The massive cranes of the Fairview Container Terminal where I spent the past two years waiting for something, anything, to happen. When he put me there the boss told me the anti-terror squad was a glamour gig. It's not. Halifax is the first port of call for millions of tonnes of U.S.-bound cargo. That means nasty guys with bad intentions might just try to slip a surprise through the container terminals here. Thus the squad. Two years, no dirty bombs, no terror plots and, until today, no yellow tape flapping in the breeze.

I pulled my badge out and showed it to some rookie with a clipboard standing guard beside one of the cruisers. He logged the number. Guess it hadn't expired. I ducked under the line and back in time. Couldn't help smiling. Walking into a real crime scene again, owning it. Blair would shoot me between the eyes if he caught that smile. My partner was getting soft on the routine of the task force detail. Maybe I was too. We used to be real cops, solved our fair share of murders. Now the boss liked to say we were in the business of preventing mass murder, not solving individual ones. It's what he said when we got bored with task force duty. He said it a lot.

There was a dead guy face down in the mud. He was naked and his hands were locked behind his back. Like I said, murder. Carla Cage was crouched beside the body. She was the best in the forensics game. Having her here was a break.

"Hey, Sergeant."

"Cam. You slumming?" She glanced my way and then turned her attention back to the vic.

"Took the call just like you." I pulled out a notebook and jotted down a few first impressions. Show the good Sergeant I was in the game. She looked over again.

"Really? Guess the horseshoe finally fell. Give me a minute and this one is all yours." She lingered on the all. I didn't like that. Didn't much like the horseshoe shot either. Cops call the anti-terror task force the golden horseshoe squad. Our horseshoes were said to be lodged in a very uncomfortable place. Lucky us.

"Sure, Sarge, take what you need. I'll look for that horseshoe."

I walked up a steep mound of hard-packed clay to stand above the scene. The body was beside a service road that wound its way to the top of the old dump. Thirty years ago the city realized the harbourfront wasn't a wise place to bury its garbage and closed the place. They covered everything in clay and hoped for the best. I watched Sergeant Cage work the body for a few seconds before turning away. I'd carry the dead guy with me for the rest of my life and wasn't ready to pick him up just yet.

I looked down at the container terminal. Could the victim be connected to the billion-dollar flood of goods that rode the tides into the port every year? I'd have to answer that question quickly. A murder outside the port gates is just a murder, inside it is an international incident.

The squeal of steel on steel rose from the terminal. Its acres of concrete held thousands of colourful inter-modal containers. All of them, it seemed, in motion. Gantry cranes sat where the concrete met the waterline. They pulled containers from the decks of ships tied to the dock. Forklifts hauled away the steel containers as fast as the cranes lowered them to the concrete. Each container moving toward the waiting trains and trucks that would feed them into the voracious consumer market that is North America.

I looked at the fence wrapped around the terminal lot. Towers rose above its corners. They held cameras, lights, motion sensors, even heat sensors. All the gadgets a paranoid society was willing to pay for, just to sleep at night. There were supposed to be sensors here in the dump too. How the hell did a dead body land beside such a secure bit of real estate? There'd be hell to pay for that. Might be mine to pay. On the upside, that dead body got me out of the terminal and back into the world. Now to stay out.

I turned back to the vic and saw Blair Christmas stomping up the hill. At six foot four he pushed the scales to two hundred and sixty pounds. None of it jiggled. He moved quickly with long strides, his coal black shoulder-length hair swinging with each step. His deep-set eyes scanned left and right as he walked. Brilliant white teeth blinked through a broad smile. I'd seen men mistake that smile for softness. They were left picking up their own teeth. My partner was not subtle.

"Don't think I've ever been on this side of the fence," he said.

"Me either. Someone might make an issue of that now," I said.

"Can't see it. We keep the guns, bombs and terrorists out of the containers. What happens out here, not our problem." He stood beside me and turned his gaze to the body below.

"You keep telling yourself that," I said.

He had a point. Unless the dead guy was sprinkled with anthrax or had an "Al-Quaeda Rocks" tattoo, he probably wasn't our problem. I didn't want him to be a terrorist but I did want him to be our problem.

"Let's just play cop a bit. Find any clues?" I asked.

"Nope. The dockworker who found the body is in the clear though and I got us a time line. That help?" The smile again.

"Let's have it."

"Okay. I talked to Billy Oikle, you remember him. He found our recently departed." He gestured toward the body. "Guy worked thirty years down there before retiring last month. Now he spends every morning and evening prowling the perimeter keeping an eye on what he calls the slackers inside. You believe that? Guy needs a hobby," Blair said.

"He mean us?"

"Nope. The guys on the cranes. He says we'd have to do some work before he'd call us slackers. Meant it too."

"Longshoremen. Bull work or no work." We'd heard it for two years.

"Yep. Anyway, says he left at sunset last night and was back at sunrise today. Security guys at the gate know him well and say that fits with his pattern," Blair explained.

"They see him leave last night? They see anything at all?"

"Patience, partner. Day-shift guys just know his routine. They weren't here last night. The night-shift guys are on the way back in to talk to us. Anyway, I called his wife and she confirmed he came home at about nine o'clock and didn't leave again until this morning. He tells me there was no dead guy here when he left last night so there's our time frame."

Carla Cage walked up the hill. A beauty in a baggy blue body suit and booties. A matching hood covered her hair and most of her face. Haute crime scene. Ravishing.

"Hi, Blair. Nice to see you. Cam, the body's free now. Coroner will give you an exact cause, but I can tell you he was strangled and stabbed and there is no sign of a weapon. If it's here, though, we'll find it." She nodded toward a team of officers in identical body suits fanning out with metal detectors. Hard to tell if the body suits were to keep them from contaminating the crime scene or keep the dump from contaminating them.

"Hey there, Sarge. Great to see you." Blair's smile broadened. He's like that.

"Thanks, Sergeant," I said.

"Good luck, gents, you'll need it on this one." She smiled broader than Blair, turned and walked away. Go figure.

Time to visit the star of the show. The dead man looked to be in his late fifties, hard to tell for sure without seeing his face. We'd get to that, no rush. I squatted low beside the body as Blair moved around to the other side. I needed time with the victim, so did he. We fell into the old pattern easily. Tomorrow we would have pictures and notes but nothing beat a fresh corpse. This guy had a story to tell and we were hear to listen.

His hands were tied together with plastic flex cuffs. The kind riot cops use. Electricians also carry them for bundling cables so I wasn't going to haul in the riot squad just yet. I pulled a pen from my pocket and tapped it on the plastic. Tight, no wriggle room at all. The victim's right hand was above his left, both palms up. His arms were locked straight back, his hands at the base of his spine. The sun glinted off a gold band. Next of kin notification would begin with a newly minted widow.

There was bruising along the upper back and shoulders. I

figured someone moved the body after death. Bruises and scrapes marked his elbows as well. It looked as though he had been on his back with his arms cuffed and pinned beneath him at or near the time of death. The coroner would have the final word on that, but I made the note. Darker marks ran across the back of his neck. I could feel my shoes sink into the mud as I leaned forward to check them out. The man was not quite face down in the mud, his head was turned slightly to the right, toward Blair. I could see the marks on the back of the neck changed from bruising to cuts toward the front.

"Well shit." Blair stood quickly and moved away from the body.

"What's up?"

"I think we should get back inside the fence and chase terrorists. Now."

If I didn't know better I'd say the big guy was afraid of something. I moved around the body.

"Blair, tell me that's not...." I swallowed, couldn't bring myself to say the name.

"Sorry, bud, that is, or was, Pastor Sandy Gardner. The great man himself. The saviour of the lost children," Blair said.

"Fuck." I moved away and joined Blair.

"Well said."

Sandy Gardner's face was recognizable, even dead and coated in dried mud. The bushy brown moustache, matching eyebrows and famous dimpled chin. The small L-shaped scar on the right cheek sealed it. I turned back toward the terminal entrance. Sandy Gardner's face smiled back from a billboard across the street. Nice tan, no mud. Brown eyes glistened beneath those eyebrows, the scar and dimple prominent. The dead Sandy Gardner's eyes didn't glisten at all. The bigger-than-life Sandy Gardner was surveying his domain from above. The lifeless pastor surveyed nothing. The billboard text invited wayward souls to come home to the Church of Salvation. Gardner worked the bible-thumping big leagues. He ran an adoption agency from his Church of Salvation office. He sliced red tape with a God-powered light sabre, bringing third-world children to new homes in North America with little or no delay. A global TV audience tuned in to Pastor Gardner's weekly services. Donations poured in and the orphans kept coming. The healing power of TV. I caught Carla Cage's eye. She smiled. Cute. She probably kicked kittens too.

"Relax, Blair, this is no hand-me-down from major crime. Too hot. They'll never give it to us." No longer sure I wanted him to be our problem. Hell of a case if we could crack it. Suicide if we couldn't.

"Sure. I can see the line forming out in the parking lot now. This town is lousy with cops wanting this case," he said.

"Hmm," was all I had for him.

I walked over to Carla Cage hoping I didn't look as sick as I felt. No point in ruining my rep as a frosty cop.

"You better break out the tent poles and canvas, Sergeant. Cover him up, we won't be moving him any time soon."

"Expecting rain, Cam?"

"Some kind of storm, yeah."

"Locusts would be biblically appropriate, I guess."

"Was thinking of something a little earthier."

That smile again. I thought punching her in the nose would be unprofessional so I headed back to join Blair and Sandy Gardner instead.

SNAKE HOWARD'S BLONDE HAIR twisted in his wake. It slapped his leather-covered shoulders just above his patch. A demonic red face filled his back, the blonde hair danced around blue flames rising from its horns. Satan. Snake pulled the clutch lever into the handlebar and stomped a heavy leather boot on the shifter rod. The fifteen Satan's Stallions following their president downshifted as one. The parade of big bikes slowed, their engines backfiring and coughing. A parked car's alarm squealed against the rumble as the bikes passed. As vice president and sergeant-at-arms, Gunner rode beside and slightly behind Snake. He grabbed the pearl-handled pistol grip that topped the suicide shifter beside his gas tank. His left boot pushed and released the foot clutch as he shoved the pistol forward. His bike popped and banged with the rest. He gave the throttle a quick twist and rolled up wheel to wheel with Snake. He pointed to the police cars beside the container terminal ahead. Snake held up two fingers and nodded, the club president then kicked his bike down another gear setting off the backfiring and popping again as the procession slowed with him. Gunner grabbed a handful of brake and forced his bike to a quick stop at the shoulder of the road. He shoved his shifter until the neutral light glowed green beneath his speedometer.

He planted his boots on the pavement and turned to watch his brothers. The Satan's Stallion Motorcycle Club was an ominous spectacle, even to a born-to-it Stallion like Gunner. He tasted the exhaust in the air. He felt the road tremble beneath his boots as the parade rolled past. The club name arched shoulder to shoulder at the top of each man's back. Letters in red surrounded by ice blue. Beneath it Satan grinned. At the bottom curved upward, the rocker that named their territory, Halifax. Air-brushed blue skulls bathed in flames marked most gas tanks. Barbed wire lined a few others. SFFS could be seen on every bike. Stallion Forever Forever Stallion, brother. Jimmy Williams, his greasy locks trailing back in the wind, rode the final bike in the group. A radically raked trike with two wide skins in back and one skinny-ass tire stretched way out front. Williams wore a prospect's patch, the mark of a rider still trying to earn full club membership. He had Halifax curved along the bottom of his back but no Satan's head above it. Gunner signalled for Williams to join him. The trike pulled in behind Gunner's bike and stopped. Neither man spoke.

The Stallion train rolled on, making a left turn at the bottom of the hill beneath the smiling face of Sandy Gardner. The bikers rode between the posts supporting the billboard and past a slowly opening steel gate into the club compound. His club safe at home, Gunner jammed his left foot into the clutch and shoved the shifter lever forward without saying a word to Jimmy Williams. He rolled ahead and turned his bike away from the clubhouse and into the parking lot of the old dump. He twisted his right hand hard and opened the throttle. The big bike howled and slewed violently and then straightened as he raced across the lot, stopping just short of the yellow police tape. The trike carrying Jimmy Williams screeched to a halt beside Gunner. The two let their bikes idle at a deep rumble as a cop walked over.

"What's with all the yellow tape?" Gunner asked the young policeman.

"You should just move along." The cop rested his hand on top of his holstered gun as he glanced back over his shoulder.

"Back down, boy. We're not here for trouble. Don't you start any." Gunner smiled. He liked fear, especially in a cop.

"Leave the area. Now," the cop said.

"Fuckin' cops," Jimmy said.

"Look man, keep your hand away from your fuckin' gun. We just want to know what's up. This is our neighbourhood," Gunner said.

He placed his hands on the handlebars in front of him, making sure the cop could see them and gestured for Jimmy to do the same. Not exactly raising their hands in surrender, just relaxing. Fear was fun but outlaw bikers also make cops twitchy. No point in giving this guy an excuse to do something stupid. Gunner's smile returned as the officer stared at the blood red tattoos on his neck. FTW rose from his left shoulder to his ear. FTP matched it on the right side. Fuck the world, fuck the police.

Jimmy Williams' bare arms showed more ink than a daily newspaper. His hatred of the young officer was more than skin deep. Gunner stood well over six feet tall but it was Williams at only four foot three who had the cop shaking. The little man on the trike was smouldering and the police officer would have to be dead not to feel the hate.

THE HEAVY METAL SYMPHONY from across the street drew me away from the late Sandy Gardner. I turned to watch Snake lead the Satan's Stallion into the club compound. I was ten the first time I saw and heard an outlaw formation, seventeen the first time I rode in one. Something about it still pulled hard. I knew better now but it still made me twitch. I saw Gunner lead a trike into the parking lot and pull up next to the rookie standing guard at the police line. I saw the rookie make the move with his right hand. Looking for comfort from the gun. Never say things can't get worse. I looked back down at Sandy Gardner's lifeless form. He'd wait. I headed to the parking lot, might as well avoid an increase in the body count.

I placed a hand on the rookie's shoulder as I moved past him. I could feel his posture relax. I moved toward the bikes, reached over the elevated handlebars on Gunner's bike and pushed the kill switch beside the throttle. The big engine died. I glanced at Jimmy Williams; the little man on the trike looked down and killed his engine. I grabbed Gunner's extended right hand, pulled him forward on the bike and embraced him, slapping his patch with my left hand as we hugged.

"You harassing the troops again?" I asked as I stepped back.

"Felt the other way around." He spoke to me but gave the young patrolman a hard stare. "Why you bringing your gang into our territory?"

"Gunner, this whole city is my territory. I just let you ride in it. Now what drags you out of bed at this hour?" I asked, moving to stand between him and the uniformed officer.

"Haven't been to bed yet."

I looked over toward Jimmy Williams and smiled.

"Officer, do you have a breathalyser unit in your car? I think I smell alcohol off this one," I said.

"Fuckin' cops," Jimmy muttered.

"What? I'm not your hero anymore, Jimmy?" I asked.

"Fuck you," he answered.

"Don't say a word, prospect," Gunner said. "This isn't the cage, Cam. Your hero days ended when you crawled in with that crowd." Gunner nodded toward the officers beyond the yellow tape.

All work on the crime scene had stopped. Every eye on the parking lot. I could feel the hate flow through me in both directions. Once again I stood between the bikers and the badge. That movie was getting old. Best to end the reunion.

"Unless you have something to share about the dead man over there, you should head to the clubhouse, big brother. Tell Snake I'll be over to speak with all of you shortly."

"Not coming in behind a badge, Cam. Who's the stiff?" Gunner asked.

"Go away, Gunner. Tell your fearless leader I want to take a look at the club surveillance tapes. His co-operation would be appreciated."

"Well, look what we have here." Blair arrived, looking to toss some fuel on a fire I had under control. Always perfect timing, my partner.

"We rarely get to see actual criminals at a crime scene. Care to confess, lowlife?" he said to Jimmy Williams.

"Fuckin' cops." Williams turned away from Gunner as he said it.

"Brilliant retort there, tiny. Show me the papers on that tricycle," Blair said.

"Not now, partner." I said. "They're leaving. Like I said. Take off, Gunner."

Gunner reached down to the right and moved the kick-start pedal out from the bike's engine. He kept his eyes on the young patrolman as he jumped into the air and came down on it hard. The big engine exploded back to life. He rolled off to the left in a hard turn. The bike leaned as though it would drop to the pavement before he twisted the throttle and the engine's torque pulled it upright and away. Williams followed close behind. The horned demon's head stared back from Gunner's patch. Williams seemed to have horns of his own.

I turned toward the patrolman and looked at the name tag on his kevlar vest. Kid was maybe twenty-two.

"Constable Barber, you reach for that gun you better plan to pull it and if you pull it you better be ready to use it. That High Noon shit will get you or someone else killed. Clear?"

"Yes, sir." He looked at the ground.

"You know, Cam," Blair said as we moved away, "just because he's your brother doesn't mean you have to be nice to his friends."

"I know. But if this was Stallion business, they wouldn't be here asking questions and the body wouldn't be so easy to find. Besides, if the clubhouse wasn't underneath his billboard they wouldn't know who Sandy Gardner was. Probably still don't."

I looked up. The beaming paper pastor smiled agreement as the bikes rolled beneath him through the clubhouse gate. I headed back to the real thing. No beaming going on there.

"Well, let's go grab this career-ender with both hands and see what kind of shit we can shake out of it." Why not.

"Great idea," Blair muttered. "Can't imagine a better plan."

Mira Milk Run

MARY STEELE

I PEERED THROUGH the frosty kitchen window in time to see familiar black letters speed past the end of the driveway. The milk truck was right on schedule.

A twinge of apprehension touched my mind at the thought of leaving my children unattended. But a quick glance around the living room showed that the baby was asleep in his playpen and the four-year-old was enthralled by dancing numbers on the TV screen. I reminded myself that it took mere minutes to retrieve the milk crate from the end of the driveway and that I'd be back before I was even missed.

In the summertime, living on top of a hill overlooking Mira Gut made me feel like "Queen of the Mira," but in the winter I could appreciate how isolated Rapunzel must have felt in her tower.

I slipped into my jacket and boots, scooted out the kitchen door, and picked my way across the ice to the snowdrifts beside the driveway. Once winter wrapped its icy fingers around the hill, the only way up or down was through the snowdrifts.

Six steps down the hill I found myself teetering in hip-deep snow. I grabbed at the tips of nearby bushes for balance but fell face first in the powdery snow. Twigs poked into my clothing and hair. A few scratched my face. Snow seeped into my fleece-lined boots and promptly began to melt.

By the time I reached the birch tree at the bottom of the

driveway, I was cold, wet, and indignant.

I looked up the hill and counted the number of inverted snow angels that marked my descent like a trail of bread crumbs. Wearily, I dropped down beside the milk crate and dug slush from my boots as I mulled over my options for the return trip.

I decided on a frontal assault. If I used the few bare spots and rock protrusions for footholds, I should be able to pick my steps up the ice-covered driveway. The weight of the milk crate and its cargo would give me the added traction I needed to succeed.

The first twenty feet went well. Then my foot slipped off the tiny rock serving as my grip, and suddenly I was sliding backwards down the driveway on my hands and knees, being chased by the blue milk crate, which was rapidly gaining on me.

Finally my knees ran aground on some bare gravel and I came to an abrupt and painful halt. I reached out and grabbed the speeding crate as it passed me on its way down the hill. With the other hand I clung to a bare rock.

A couple of deep breaths helped restore my composure but not my pride. I chuckled ruefully as I remembered a line from a poem I read in high school, "hands and knees to the coconut trees." I struggled to my feet again and glanced up the hill. I didn't see any coconut trees, just ice and snow.

I got about fifteen feet before I was again in reverse on my hands and knees being pursued by the persistent milk crate. Again a couple of pieces of gravel sticking out of the ice jolted me to a stop. Again I reached out and caught the wayward milk crate.

It was time for a change in tactics. I looked across the driveway. The distance between me and the snowdrifts was covered with smooth, flawless ice. I'd never cross it without breaking my neck or my skull or some other necessary bone in my body.

Perhaps I should *crawl* up the hill. With two hands and two knees to anchor myself, I should have twice the chance of success.

A crow interrupted my thoughts as he called from high in a

nearby maple tree. I glanced up as he spread his wings and cawed again. He was probably laughing at me. I hoped he was the only one. I glanced around quickly—not a car in sight, not a person in sight, no one in a distant window watching my humiliation. I was alone with my battered ego and the crate of milk. Eager to be upright before someone happened along, I returned to my task.

The crate complicated matters considerably. I shoved it ahead of me as if playing shuffleboard, and crawled after it as far as I could until gravity stepped in and sent it after me. I continued in this manner, gaining ten feet and losing four, until at last I planted my foot firmly on a patch of snow at the summit. The milk run had lasted much longer than usual.

I had visions of the baby crying and the four-year-old confused and upset as he watched his mother's plight from the window. Clutching the milk crate, I hobbled to the doorway and limped inside, prepared to comfort my anxious children.

My four-year-old didn't even glance toward the kitchen as I closed the back door and took off my coat and boots. Instead, he sat glued to the TV screen as Sesame Street characters sang the virtues of the number 12. The baby was still asleep.

Silently, I sank onto a kitchen chair. My fingers and toes began to sting as the warm air touched them. That was when I noticed dots of blood scattered across my palms where skin used to be.

I turned the oven to 500 degrees, poured a cup of strong, steaming tea, and propped my feet up on the open oven door.

The heat from the oven warmed my toes; the tea warmed my insides and contentment warmed my soul. It felt good to be indispensable.

Miranda

MAUREEN HULL

WEDNESDAY, 10 P.M.: She will be sorry in the morning if she doesn't go to bed now, but she can't settle. She putters around the kitchen after Trip goes to bed, making the fishing lunch, wiping the counters. She checks the weather report again. If it's calm they might bring a few trawls ashore tomorrow. There are three days left in the season. She pinches dead leaves from her neglected plants. Jesse's at a friend's for the night; Zoe's asleep; Shelly's God-knows-where with the new boyfriend. Miranda doesn't want to think about what they might be doing. It's a school night, and Shelly's curfew is ten-thirty.

Three cars swish by in front of the house. There is a big pothole in front of their driveway and the culvert doesn't drain properly. Trip is counting on another election soon, so the road crew will fill in the hole and clean the culvert before it backs up and floods the basement. Miranda hopes the boyfriend—what's his name? Sean?—has the sense to slow down in the rain. Trip is sprawled over most of the bed. She can move him and disturb his sleep, or she can go crawl into Jesse's bed. Cranky captain in the boat tomorrow versus cold bed. She chooses the cold bed. She sleeps lightly, rising to semi-awareness every time a vehicle drives by, waking when one stops in the yard. She squints at Jesse's Spiderman clock: 2 a.m.

"Do you know what time it is?" she hisses over the banister

to Shelly who is sock-footing it up the stairs.

"The car broke down," Shelly hisses back. "We had to get a tow."

"You should have called."

"It's a fishing night, remember? I'm not supposed to call after nine o'clock and wake you up."

"Unless it's an emergency!"

"An emergency is when we skid into the river and they call you from the hospital!"

Trip mumbles in his sleep. Shelly and Miranda glare at one another. They both want to yell. Shelly's just about strangling to keep from it. Miranda's dying to rant, maybe even laugh. Why does she always want to laugh in the middle of arguments, when nothing's funny? But they won't risk waking Trip, not for this. They turn their backs and go to bed, each longing to slam a door. Miranda punches Jesse's pillows, shakes the duvet into submission, closes her eyes, and vibrates. She can't imagine how she'll manage in the boat. She'll probably stumble and fall overboard and drown. Shelly will be wretched with remorse. Like hell.

THURSDAY, 4:15 A.M.: Miranda pushes hard with her muscles, up and off the side of the bed. If she lingers she'll fall back asleep and then the alarm will shock her and Trip will wake up and stumble around the kitchen, in her way. She'll lose her private time. Coffee always helps, the first dark drift of it up from the pot. By the time she is halfway through her first cup she is focused on the day ahead, listening to the wind.

When she was nine, Miranda was given an illustrated book of fables. She disliked the preachy tone of the stories, and the lesson in italics at the end of each one—she wished the nasty ant would get stepped on so the merry grasshopper could inherit his stash and not die—but she liked the fable about the sun and the wind. In a contest to prove who was the strongest, they tried to make a man take off his coat. The harder the wind blew, the tighter he pulled the coat around his body. It was the sun's relentless heat that made him take off his coat. Until she went fishing for a living, she believed the sun was more powerful than the wind. Now she knows better.

A warm, sticky wind, dense with moisture, will have her stripped to her skin quicker than any fireball in the sky. And nothing is as powerful as the wind when it shows its true muscled self: a mass of energy that moves around, over, or through anything in its way. It tosses branches, trees, rocks, roofs, and boats. It slaps the sea like a child slaps bathwater, it flings skirts of hungry ocean ashore to rub away the land under summer cottages so that they fall in the water, their decks splintering and littering the coast. It drives waves to suck and draw at the edges of seaside graveyards, so that coffins stick out of cliff edges like raisins in half-eaten pudding. It heaves boulders, seaweed, driftwood, and a confetti of styrofoam buoy chips in windrows far inland.

In a gale, the house shakes with every gust. Miranda can hear five-inch spikes moaning, she can hear floorboards wanting to be trees again. Those mornings she heads straight for the weather channel, switches on the radio before she plugs in the kettle, wanting the numbers: thirty, forty, gusting to fifty. They drive to the wharf, sit in the truck and watch the boats heave and jerk. Trip rolls down his window to talk to the other fishermen. Miranda nods "good morning," but says nothing. She is supposed to be keen, to want to go in all weather, for the money for their family, but it isn't that way with her. If anything happened, she and Trip would go down together and their kids would be orphaned. She thinks they could bear the loss of one parent, but not two. She'd rather the worry of unpaid bills than the pain of imagining them growing up without Trip, and without her. If the wind blows too hard, she won't say anything but will show by her body language that she thinks they should not take the risk. They should go home.

5 A.M.: THE SUN BALLOONS RED on an indigo horizon. The sea heaves and swells, but the wind is finally asleep and a great silence covers the world. The air is clean, blown free of all dust and debris. It shimmers in the early morning light. Miranda breathes deeply, and watches the sun on the water as if for the first time. The water is gun-metal grey. The sun slides liquid yellow across it and it pools in the hollows between the swells. She can almost feel it on her gloves as she moves the dripping traps along the washboard. She half expects the lobsters to slip, buttery, out of her hands.

Everything shifts, and the ocean turns the colour of a ripe plum. The swells flatten, the sun lifts the butter from the hollows, and it melts into the air. Miranda is busier and busier: there is less and less time to notice anything outside the boat. There are bait bags to empty and refill, traps to pick and bait, lobster to measure, sort, and band. When she glances up again, the sun is incandescent, the sea sizzles with sequins, and the light breeze lifting her hair is the wind of the boat's passage as they sail from trawl to trawl. Her first season out—a cold and windy spring—she'd learned to treasure early mornings like this. They were loose gems, in a velvet pouch, tucked in a corner in her mind.

7 A.M.: TO SAIL INTO FOG is to abandon time, land, surety.

In the cabin, Trip is reading coloured bands on the screen overhead, and the scrying crystal of the compass bolted to the dash. The first tells him what the ocean floor beneath the boat is made up of and what is swimming between it and themselves; the second tells him which direction lies over which shoulder, and where they are headed. More or less.

Miranda believes the colour sounder, with its scrolling bargello tapestry, reveals a profound reality. She thinks the tiny green pin-dots, scurrying this way and that as the boat passes over them, are not so much computer shorthand for a school of fish as they are the glint of life energy in each single fish. The heavy red lines, lifting and falling, are the after-glow of the rocks, cooled down after the planet's birth. To the naked eye they look like sea bottom—grey mud, brown stone—but the sounder picks up the last remnants of their glowing hearts and blazes them across its screen.

She knows the compass lies. She is sure—gut sure—the wharf lies to the left, twenty degrees forward from the jut of her elbow. Her heart tells her where her house sits with her children asleep in their beds. The compass says that way is town, and she is eighty degrees off in her reckoning. Miranda thinks the compass spins around and changes its opinions like a dizzy girl who only wants to be popular with the boys. It particularly sucks up to Trip. With the felted walls of fog all around them, the compass can say anything and Trip will believe it.

Fog makes up all the world ten, or twenty, feet away. You can believe you are in the one clear space in the whole mass of it but, bit by bit, layer by layer, you become soaked. Under your oil gear your clothing has, inch by inch, thread by thread, drawn up the fog until it nestles next to and licks your skin. There's no separation, no twenty, or ten, feet. The fog funnels down your lungs, and into your stomach. It floats up your tear ducts and through your nasal passages and ear canals. It sneaks into your brain and befuddles it. When it tells you you are in another dimension, you believe it. When it crumples time and tosses it overboard, you don't notice. You simply wait, and wait. Eventually, things come out of the fog. Buoys. The ghost shape of another boat. A piece of decking from a dock a hundred miles down the coast. A resting gull. The wharf.

"We'll wait until it clears a bit," says Trip, nosing up to the east wharf so Miranda can jump ashore with the bowline. "I'm just wasting fuel wandering around in this." They can find their trawls well enough with the electronics, but they can't put them back in any decent order, can't see if they might be laying across someone else's gear.

"Lucky we found the wharf," says Miranda.

"No luck to it," he laughs. "I read the compass. Where's the coffee?"

Miranda knows it is luck. The compass has decided to play fair and align itself with the magnetic field long enough for Trip to find the wharf. The luck is that the compass likes Trip, and will cooperate with him.

8:30 A.M.: A SLOW DRIZZLE is coming down. Miranda thinks she might never be dry again. She will end up covered in mold; she can feel it creeping over her skin and into her brain. When it blows, it rains. When it's foggy, it rains. On a sunny day, a cloud will drift over to the boat and rain on Miranda's head. She hates rain, but she's learned to dress for it. The first few seasons she was often cold, her fingers numb and white, her feet aching stumps. When they came ashore, she'd go to bed, lie under quilts, and shiver for twenty minutes before she could fall asleep. Finally she took to wearing two pairs of wool socks and felt liners in her boots, and layers of wool sweaters under gortex and thinsulate. Some days she wears two wool toques—on really bad days she wears three. She knows what she looks like: dumpy. She doesn't give a good goddamn.

Everything falls on her: rain, snow, sleet, fish guts, herring scales. Falls down on her, blows up at her, works its way down her neck and up her sleeves. She doesn't mind so much when the catches are good—when there's plenty for her to do: baiting, measuring, banding. The day goes by in a blur and each lobster is money in their pockets. When the catches are poor, there's not enough to do. She spends too much time sitting on an upturned bucket, trying to keep low to the wind, brooding as they sail between trawls. There is little or no financial reward and nothing to be gained but fatigue and bad temper. The boat lurches and jerks in the crosstides. It's as though someone is constantly shoving her, and she never knows when or from what direction to expect it. She imagines a malevolent spirit whose gleeful pleasure it is to torture her. After a bad day in the boat the earth lurches up and down beneath her feet as she staggers along the wharf to the truck. It seems like hours before the earth is stable enough to trust again.

The fishing, the ocean, the weather, all of it—to Trip it is a challenge, a cycle, a rhythm. It's government regulations, bureaucratic bunglings, sleazy hidden political agendas that rouse his contempt, his frustration, and his anger. To Miranda, the political and economic pitfalls, tricks, and betrayals are more remote, more like unfathomable foreign languages. It's the wind, the cold, and the ocean that torment her. Cruel and remorseless—then turning sunny and sweet, gentle and teasing, like a moody, capricious lover she can't leave. Her heart melts, she's entranced with the colours, tickling breezes, rainbow spray and sun on her face. She has no defense against such beauty.

9 A.M.: THEY SAIL IN AND OUT of the wet, hauling gear. One trawl will be in the clear, the next under a fine spray hissing into the water. Miranda's face is wet and her toque is soggy. She won't wear a sou'wester, one of those rubber hats with an extended back brim, designed to send the rain off your back and away from your neck. The chin strap chafes, and the hat won't stay on in any kind of wind without it. She'd had one, the first year, had worn it a few times in the rain. The strap kept sliding out of position and got oily and disgusting from the bait residue on her gloves when she fingered it back into place. She shoved it into the bottom of the box they keep spare lobster bands in and forgot about it. Trip, like the other fishermen, wears a ball cap. If it rains he wears an oil jacket with a hood and his ball cap sticks out from under it. Tourists buy sou'westers and take them home and do God-knows-what with them. Bronze them, maybe. Plant flowers in them. Costume designers buy them

and make the fishermen in documentaries about the East Coast fishery wear them.

Miranda takes refuge in daydreams. She can pick and bait and shove traps around with the surface of her mind while the rest of it goes wandering.

"Pay attention," warns Trip.

"I am," she lies.

"No, you're not. You're in never-never land. You've got that vacant look on your face. You'll be overboard if you don't smarten up."

"Stop watching me," she says.

"Wake up or stay home, Mir. You're no help like this. I'd do better on my own."

"No, you wouldn't. You'd fall overboard and drown and I'd be a widow with three kids to raise." She'll have to sell the house and gear. She'll have to go to work, and that will mean going back to the city. The theatre will take her back, Reeve will make them. They'll be really poor, but they'll manage. Shelly can get a part-time job, and Jesse can deliver papers or something. She won't marry again, marriage is too much bloody work and, besides, she doesn't want some strange man messing with her kids. When they're grown up, she'll think about men again. Maybe she'll get married again later. Somebody with money, and a housekeeper. They'll travel to Europe. Have a place in the Bahamas. She'll be an exquisite hostess. Lose ten pounds, have a little plastic surgery. She'll have a studio with a big cutting table and bolts and bolts of silk. She'll make a faux sou'wester and hang it on her wall. Drape it with a little seaweed: dark green lace and red and white fringy stuff like Irish moss. She'll miss Trip dreadfully, never get over him really—a quiet part of her soul will always be in mourning.

"Earth to Miranda," hollers Trip. "That's the second time you've missed that buoy. I can sail up to it but I can't put it in the boat for you!"

"I barely missed it," lies Miranda. "Go around again." Guilt swamps her, makes her testy. "It's the waves, they snatch it away from the hook."

"Well, snatch it the hell back!"

Maybe she won't miss him all that much. Yes, she will, she will, she's sorry, please God, don't let him ever fall overboard. She lunges for the buoy—all of the boat hook and most of Miranda over the side.

"Jeeze, Miranda! You don't have to swim for it."

10 A.M.: IT'S AS CALM as if the water's been oiled. The rain has stopped and the fog has closed back in.

"Slack tide," says Trip. "We'll have lunch and wait, see if she lifts some." Usually the fog burns off after a few hours, but today it lingers, chilly acres of white mist. Somewhere above them, the sun is shining. Occasional rays fall down through narrow gaps and Miranda watches them hit the water, just yards away. They brighten the air but never seem to land where she is working. She would love some sun on her face. They eat lunch on deck, listening for any approaching boat who might not see them in the fog. Half the time, people don't check their radar. It's pleasant outside, cool but not cold, with the luminous light that emanates from the fog when the sun is thinning and wearing it away.

Trip sits on the engine box, she sits on an upturned bait tray, eating peanut butter sandwiches. The silence between them is as intimate as the first time they slept together and woke up together. A swell lifts the boat.

"Boat off the port side," says Trip quietly. Miranda strains to hear, then there it is: the muffled purr. "Chessie Gordon, heading for the wharf." Trip knows the sound of boat engines the way Miranda knows the sound of the children's voices along their road.

"He's done for the day," says Miranda. "He's taking his mother to the clinic this morning."

"Candy can't take her?"

"Got a ceramic class."

"You'd think she could miss it the once."

"You'd think."

"Or the old lady could take a cab."

"You'd think."

"Women."

"That supposed to get my goat?" Miranda throws her crusts at him. "You're wasting your time. I'm horny today, I don't want to fight, I want to get laid."

"You pick the damnedest times. What was wrong with last night?"

"I was exhausted."

"And now you want to? When we've still got a hundred traps to haul and the day's as slow as a snail's fart in this fog?"

"Well, not right this second. You could finish your coffee."

"You're crazy, woman. Your timing stinks."

"So does the bait. But does that put me off? Not a bit."

"You're serious, aren't you?" He's laughing.

"Take off your rubber pants, baby. Show Mama what you've got." She's laughing, too. They can't—not when they're already so late, when half the boats in the strait might be listening, when one might loom out of the fog and run into them, when everything is so damp and clumsy and there are so many layers of clothing to be got through.

A voice over Trip's shoulder says, "Move 'er to the south'ard, now."

He jumps. "Damn, that's enough to give a person a heart attack."

"It's Cranky John." Nobody calls him that to his face. He's a mile away in his boat, the *Julia-Marie*, and the fog has lifted his voice and carried it the distance. It sounds as though he is standing next to them. "Why do they call him Cranky John?"

"Sh," cautions Trip, in case the fog carries their words back.

He holds her tight to his chest and bends to kiss and whisper in her ear, "they say he's cranky all the time because Julia Marie—the wife, not the boat—won't give him any."

"That'd make me cranky," says Miranda.

He kisses her again. "Back to work. Cut that bait; haul them traps."

"Yessir, Captain Bligh, sir, yessir."

NOON: THE WEIGHTS HAVE SLIPPED DOWN the buoy line of trawl number seventeen, and Trip hasn't noticed the rope floating like a sea snake just below the surface. There is a sudden vibration, a shudder, and a thump as it spins around the shaft and stalls the engine. He puts the transmission in neutral and walks back to the stern. Miranda has hooked up a loop of the rope and is holding it in the boat with the gaff. Trip hauls on one end, then the other.

"She's hooked good." He cuts the rope and hands the free end to Miranda. "Don't let go of it."

The swell gently pulls at the rope in her hand; at the end of it is the trawl of six traps and the end buoy line. She pulls the rope through a loop tied to the nearest knee and clove-hitches it off. She wants both hands free in case Trip, bending double over the side, nothing but his ass and legs in sight, starts to go over. He never has, says he never will, but Miranda takes up a post of readiness behind him, just in case. If he starts to fall she will fling herself on him, grasping his knees or heels or whatever she can, holding them hard against the side until she can figure out how to get him hauled back in. "Just remember where the life ring is," Trip says. "You'll never be able to haul me in, I'm half your weight again." Miranda knows she could. She's done it a hundred times in her dreams. She knows exactly how it would feel, how she'd summon miraculous energy from the core of her bones.

Trip finds the buoy at the end of the wrapped line, half under the boat on the port side. He pulls it up until it comes tight. He hands it to her and then begins pulling the other end. Between them they work it back and forth, the shaft slowly turning this way and that, releasing trapped coils. At last it's free and Trip leans against the gunwale to untie the rope from the knee and splice it back to the freed buoy line. He tosses the whole thing overboard and waits until they drift off a bit. The buoy dips and spins, a slow unwinding in the rising tide.

1:00 P.M.: THE CRABS GET MORE STUBBORN as the day winds down. She rips a squinty-eyed devil out of a trap and only half of it comes. She's left holding a carapace: the shell-less crab, still in the trap, waves its limbs feebly. She tries to be more careful with the next one. She wants to be done with this and get home, have a hot shower, talk to Shelly and make some kind of peace before bedtime.

The propeller winds itself in rope, again, and it takes Trip fifteen minutes to work it free. She misses another buoy and they sail back around to try again. More time wasted. While Trip sails out to the last set of trawls she digs around in the lunch box for a cookie. She picks the chocolate chips out, eats them, and throws the rest of the cookie overboard. "Shelly didn't get in until after two. We had a fight."

"I didn't hear anything."

"We whispered. It was a whisper fight."

"I can't tell you how much I appreciate that."

"She said the car broke down."

Miranda catches the next two buoys handily, she credits the steadying effect of the chocolate. The hauler strains and screeches. They have two traps up, and the rest won't come.

"Snagged on something."

The third trap labours to the surface, the hauler whining. Miranda sees net floating.

"Ghost net." Trip is disgusted. "Balled up with a load of

crap. Must be an anchor still dragging on it. Give her a shot of reverse."

Miranda goes forward and puts the boat in reverse, gives it some fuel.

"Again," he says, and the boat moves backward, the hauler grasps the slack and heaves again. The net comes slowly up and Trip starts to haul it over the gunwale. "Jesus Christ!" He jumps back.

"What?"

"Grab the boat hook," he yells, "and give me a hand."

She joins him at the side, boat hook in hand. "Dear God!" she whispers. They grab onto opposite sides of the bundle. The hauler howls like a banshee as they heave the mess into the boat.

"He's been dead awhile," says Trip. They step back, unwilling to look, unable to look away. "Don't touch anything."

He hurries into the cabin to call the RCMP. Her legs feel wrong—boneless—and she sits on the engine box, upwind, and takes several deep breaths. The sun glints on the wet netting wrapped around and around. Some of the mesh has sunk deep into the rotting fabric and flesh beneath. The wind shifts and she gags. It's worse than the half-rotted seal Jesse found one April morning on the beach below their house. Worse than the freezer when the power went out the winter they went to Toronto for two weeks. One foot is gone, bare leg bones thrust through the net. There isn't much face left. The jaws gape open, there are teeth. It is the frantic blue rictus of her nightmares.

"We're meat," she says. "We're just rotten meat."

"They'll be here in half an hour," he says. The radio crackles. Trip has been overheard by the few boats still out on the water.

"Jury-Rig 2," they call. "You on channel, Trip?" They want information. They will want to know who it is. Trip doesn't respond. He holds Miranda and waits for the RCMP....

By the time the Mounties have been and gone, taking away their statements and the sad corpse stuffed into a body bag, the sun is far to the west. They are rarely so late on the water. Trip unhooks the trawl line from the cleat he'd secured it to and shoves the two traps on the gunwale back into the water. They sail around, pick up the trawl again, and haul all the traps on board. Trip unties the buoys and hands them to Miranda to put aside. Together they cut out the heads and cut off the gates. Trip takes a hatchet and cuts the snoods—the short lengths of rope that tie the traps to the trawl line. Then he coils all the line and puts it into a garbage bag. Miranda gathers the cut-out heads—the net walls and corridors that make up the interiors of the traps—puts them into the bag and puts it beside the buoys. Trip ties the gates together and lays them on top of the garbage bag. It will all go to the dump.

Silently, they push the stripped traps overboard. No one will ever use anything from this ill-favoured trawl again. You'd never catch any fish in it again, and if you did, you'd pay for it with the worst sort of luck. Miranda doesn't want anything more to do with this trawl, any more than Trip does. Any more than any fisherman would. The empty, open traps will settle on the bottom to be cleaned and absolved. Shellfish and seaweed will cling to the wire mesh, small fish will swim in and out, feeding, or sheltering inside when large predators swim by.

There are two trawls left to haul.

Trip turns the boat around. "Let's go home," he says.

*F*lowers of *D*espair

VICTOR SAKALAUSKAS

"*I* AM NOT GOING TO HAVE ANY MORE TROUBLE out of you tonight, am I?" he said, tapping out each word on my forehead with his finger.

"No trouble, no sir, Officer," I said, thinking Fuck you. It's my house, I'll do what I want.

They came back after I upset the table and put my fist through the wall.

"You're a drunk, always will be a drunk," Cindy said, slamming the door behind me.

That was two months ago.

Now I have this one-bedroom apartment on a dead Queen corner (Victoria and Regent) in Jubilee Mines. The kids helped me take some things from the house, bedsheets, towels and dishes, the flea market junk. The 13-inch from my rec room with an almost straightened coat hanger stuck in the back for reception. The Sally Ann gave me a table and chairs. I bought a ten-dollar microwave at a yard sale that works for two minutes then stops with a puff of black smoke. Her #1 Teacher coffee mug, a Christmas gift from her students, found its way into the garbage bag containing my clothes.

I always said I married up. She was one of those teenagers looking for a bad boy. We married at a commune in PEI called "Butterflies Are Free," then drove to Montreal for a Stones concert, high on hash and magic mushrooms. My only memory of the concert is Cindy sitting on my shoulders flashing her boobs to the band. Married me in spite of her father, a church fly who saw the devil in me. If nothing else, this separation has stopped him rolling over in his grave.

After losing my license—driving while intoxicated; hate the way that sounds, nasty and formal at the same time—life turned bad. Can't be a long haul trucker (class of '86) without a license. I showed her an article that said the yeast in beer actually fights cancer. That rolled like a flat tire. Cindy asked me once why I drink. The answer is simple; I like it. How the frosty bottle fits in my hand, the bubbles inside, the icy sweat outside. The colour, the smell, the taste as it embraces my tongue like a cold lover. There is always a feeling of satisfaction and, later, calmness.

"Billy," she said. "I'm tired. Tired of your drinking. Tired of you gone all the time. And now I'm tired of you being here."

Sitting at the kitchen table as calm as a monk after meditation and she comes out with that. So I turned over the table, for the second time. What did she expect? She has this restraining order against me now, for one fucking phone call.

Haven't had a drink in one month twenty-one days. I sleep at night now and my hands have stopped trembling. And just to prove to Cindy my will power, I keep a twenty-four of Molson's in the cupboard. Some nights I park down the street from the house, walk into the backyard and sit at the picnic table. Have a smoke and stare at her bedroom window. I think about her and the kids, Sean and Michelle. I miss them.

I now share my life with rusted car bodies and dogs barking late at night. A drug dealer lived here before me, his customers still come around. Late at night knocking on the door, saying things like, "Weasel, you in there, Weasel? Open the fuckin' door."

Across the street is this old two-story house turned into apartments. Upstairs lives a fat red-headed woman. She has a son about four years old, Tyrone. He has dark skin and black curly hair. The kid plays on the street with Red out the window screaming in a voice like my Jake brakes, "You stupid little bastard. Monkey idiot. Get in this house now."

When she sees the neighbours watching, she says, "Don't play on the street, dear."

Calling Social Services moved it indoors. Where if I keep my windows closed and can't hear the screams, I can fool myself into thinking life is good.

On Friday nights at nine o'clock, the Handi-Trans bus drops off two men at Red's apartment. A fat man in a wheelchair called Boogie Board takes each step on his butt, pushing himself up backwards by his glove-covered hands. His friend Francis, with head and eyebrows shaved, has both legs bent in towards each other at the knees. They touch with every step. It's a weekend of Metallica, pizza delivery, and the smell of marijuana. Sunday they take Tyrone to the corner store for ice cream. She hugs and tells him how she loves him. I remember taking my girls to the Tasty Treat. They always ordered chocolate sundaes while we had butterscotch.

One night Boogie Board and his wheelchair tumbled down the stairs with Francis standing at the top like a gnarled, rooted tree. The next day Francis moved in and Red noticeably mellowed.

It was a hot dry summer with waves of suffocating heat rising from the asphalt. The lack of water turning lawns to dust, with mowers creating devils. Then this morning Hurricane Alice strikes. It is a welcome relief from the heat.

The hurricane brings wind, rain and Red to my door.

"Can ya drive me to the food bank? I can pay ya."

She holds out a wet crumpled five. Water drips from her T-shirt where a large red tongue flops between her huge boobs. Below are black stretch pants adorned with large white flowers. She wears pink flip-flops where sunflowers bloom around her toes. She is a garden!

This close makes her shorter and wider than I thought. The damp smell forces me to take a step back.

"Ah, yeah, sure I can drive you. I have to get my jacket."

When I come back, she still has her hand out with the money.

"You don't have to pay me."

She stuffs the five in the waistband of her pants.

I have this '88 Ford Escort—Cindy has the Explorer. Sometimes it will not start when it's damp. I cross my fingers but it starts. I take the back streets hoping no one will recognize me.

"Thanks, Mister," she says. "Thursday is food bank day. Ya got to get there early or they run out of the good stuff. Vegetables. I get loads."

Grey sheets of water close us off from everything. Leaves and small branches break from trees and litter the streets. Roads quickly flood making them almost impassable. I roll the window down to get some air and the rain slants across my face. The Escort is a standard shift and my hand brushes against her leg. I stay in second gear.

The food bank is in the old railway station made of brick, plywood windows, and security alarm. A six-foot wire fence separates the building from the rusty tracks. To help at the bank you have to belong to a church, any church. Anglican, Catholic, and Mormon—they are all there. When we arrive, two men are standing in the doorway just out of the rain. They stare at us as Red opens the door, puts her right hand on the roof and pulls herself out. The rain beats against my face making my eyes blink.

"A lot of rain," I shout.

The men say nothing. I look at the railway tracks and the woods beyond, distorted by the rain on the glass. I try again.

"I'm not with her. I'm just the driver. She needed a drive." They talk to themselves and laugh. I close the window thinking I may get my reward in heaven but I could use a Molson's now.

Red comes out. Behind her, two young men in white shirts

and tie carry boxes of food. White, blond and so clean even the rain seems to purify them. They put the groceries in the back seat, give her a card and me a look.

"She's not with me," I whisper.

Driving back to her apartment, she reads the card: "When the end comes, will you be ready?" She crumples and tosses it to the floor.

"Me, I'm just gettin' by," Red continues. "Me and Francis, that's me boyfriend, you've seen him."

She glances at me. A crooked smile pulls at her lips.

"We're thinking about gettin' married. Bigger cheque. Bigger cheque equals flat screen."

She laughs.

"That's what Francis says. He's a funny guy. Maybe they'll set us up in a house. My parents have been livin' in a welfare house for twenty years now."

Leaves catch under the wipers, leaving wet streaks on the window. I drive slowly through submerged streets wishing for a tsunami to take me away.

"Well here we are, thanks Mister, can ya carry them in for me?"

"I have to get back, it's...."

"It won't take long. Francis can't carry nothin'."

Halfway up the stairs she stops. Behind, carrying the groceries, I stop inches away from her large dimpled butt. She leans on the wall; her breathing comes in long raspy moans as if it's her last.

The top of the stairs opens into a large room. An outdoor patio set with the umbrella up is in front of a window. Wallpaper, pictures, curtains—everything sunflowers. Tyrone sits on the floor watching Wile E. Coyote falling off the edge of a cliff holding a sign that reads "OOPS." Red tosses him a box of Kellogg's Corn Flakes.

"Here ya go Tyrone."

Francis sits at the table looking out the window with a toke in his hand. He rests his elbows on the table moving his head in to take a puff. He holds the smoke in until he coughs, and then blows it to the dark cloud of smoke caught in the umbrella above his head. He always wears a black muscle shirt. His skinny arms white and hairless. On the front in yellow letters "God Is Busy Can I Help You." He slowly turns and stares at me. He turns back and looks straight down across the street into my window.

"You like watching people, don't you? I see you there, peeking from behind your curtain. You some kind of pervert or one of them nosy pricks always running to the cops."

He stands and comes towards me. Strapped to his legs are metal braces that clang with every step. The smell of marjiuana and sweat cover me as he leans in. His eyes are a dark blue, almost black.

"If you don't mind your own fuckin' business, I'll visit you some night. Some night when you're asleep. Then you'll have something to report."

One of his braces hits against my left knee. I feel the cold steel through my pant leg.

Back in my apartment, after a shower, I sit in my boxers listening to the traffic outside. I hold a beer in my right hand and watch my reflection in the TV. I have to get out of here. I'll buy Cindy flowers and we can talk, calmly. Whatever it takes. My hand trembles as I put the bottle to my lips.

*P*arallel *R*ule

TERESA O'BRIEN

*I*T IS THE SORT OF NIGHT when you would love to go swimming. Not in a blue chlorinated pool but from a gently shelving beach into the dark buoyant saltiness of the sea. Just about four feet of viscous water holding you safe and cool in the velvet night. The sort of night when even at this hour, ten thirty, the temperature still in the twenties, the air sultry and still, you might expect someone to pull into the driveway. One of Joey's friends, maybe Brad in his Dad's sports car, with the roof down. My friend Jessie with cold Coronas or a bottle of wine, although when I think about it, I haven't seen her in weeks.

There is laughter drifting over from neighbours' stoops, along with the smoke from backyard fires. It's the sort of night when nobody wants to go to bed and I am sitting on my own in the dark. While you, Joey, are lying lonely and heartbroken in your bed. I light the Coleman lamp, settle the globe. A moth swims up to the flame and I swat it away. It returns insistently, pale wings glimmering in the light. Dew falls. Chimneys disappear. Saplings play against the shed wall, frisking their leaves. On the second story your blind is drawn and there is no light in your room. I know you are awake, your body drawn white and tight against another night.

It has been four days since the phone call.

Time to get on with my life, you said. If she doesn't decide soon...if she doesn't call.

You hadn't known, of course. Had not known what it would be like.

Is Joey there?

Hold on, I'll get him for you.

Yeah, well, that's it then.

You said nothing to me except, with a shrug, it's over. The words, the gesture lying nonchalance. The days in bed, prostrate with grief, the truth. All winter and spring you had fought to keep her. There had been days when you truly believed that you would. And others, when you were not sure. Your treading-water days, I called them. Neither coming nor going. Neither living nor dead. A half life. Dissolved now into shallow breathing, the smell of sweat, the odour of bad breath.

The dog is under your bed. He raises an eyebrow, is still, then closes his eyes. And waits.

Today is warm. There is a stickiness in the air that is sickening. In your room, you have thrown off the duvet and a sheet is draped about you. On the street by the coffee shop your friends slouch in silky basketball shorts and muscle shirts. Gold chains glint in the sun. Their young boys' strut. Their fierce tattoos and piercings and their gentle hearts. A car skids to a halt in a shriek of tires and pounding music and they lean forward eagerly, then pile into the back. They have stopped calling for you.

I have barbecued scallops. Made spanakopita. I could be Philip Roth's mother. Or J.D. Salinger's. Eat. You must eat. Get out of your room. Get some fresh air. And then angrily I think, face the consequences. But I don't say that.

In the dim flickering light I eat alone. There is no irritating wind. No cold breeze. No whine of mosquitoes. No blip from my cell phone to tell me that a text has come in. Nothing to disturb except that blinded window. And beyond it like the touch of my skin, like the mole I worry on my left wrist, like my own breath, your body on the bed. Pale, motionless.

Photographs are traps behind every ornament, slipping from books, on the mantelpiece. You and the girl gazing intently at each other. Wide smiles unbiddable in the joy of the moment. Locked hands. Forever.

Are you pleased with yourself now, I say viciously to the girl in the photo when I pass. Are you pleased?

Sometimes I see myself in those photos. Josef's hands in my hair. Your father was good looking and passionate and transient. The looks, the passion you inherited from him, the steadfastness, which some might call boring, from me. I was not always like this. I had to struggle against that self. Took my half-charred heart through a litany of miserable rooms and proceeded to rebuild myself. A tougher version, less likely to be seared by hot breaths and lovers' fire. That's life. Get over it. Ups and downs. Because by then I had you. We were a team. Until the girl came.

I fret stupidly about the weather. Our brief summer squandered. For four days now I have brought tea, toast. But I am growing impatient. I have forgotten the pain of my charred body. The dead weight that was my burned heart. And also, there is another thing. I cannot bear your pain. I want to hold alcohol-drenched cloths to a feverish brow. I want you to be a child again so that I can make you better. There's a rage in me as I think of the girl, her slim white shoulders and narrow hips. And how the two of you used to walk, hand in hand. I think, stupidly, irrationally, why can't you be more like your father? Heartless, heartbreaker Josef. And then I think, I should have had more children and if I had five children I wouldn't even notice what they were up to half the time. But I didn't. And I do. Do notice, do notice all too well. And what does that say about me, I wonder.

I open the door, trace the hair on your unshaven face. Your arms emerge. A slight acknowledgment before they draw back to cradle yourself. I want to shake you. Shake your legs into walking.

Beat your chest until it is bruised and welts rise on your skin. Hibernating. In the fullness of summer. In full daylight.

I did not know then that you were not squandering yourself but slowly saving yourself up. I did not know that.

And so in my impatience, I draw you out of bed: your paleness against my weathered arms shocking. I urge you out of the fetid room where time has leached your face until it is the colour of your walls. Chalk. Parchment, or was it Bone White? I bring towels, bathing shorts. We will have a beach day, just like we used to when you were young. You yawn and I see a furred tongue. Your breath is stale. Your body damp with sweat.

You do not fiddle with the CD player but stare out the window. You say nothing, not even, This is stupid.

It is late in the afternoon. The water is calm and stretches brilliant blue. There are few people left on the beach. A young mother takes a last look at the sea, throws away a cigarette and gathers up plastic toys. A man carries a small dog to the water and washes off its paws. For a while you sit there, staring out to sea, and then you walk into the water. I walk beside you but stop at chest height. I am not a good swimmer. Always, I will go out so far and then swim parallel to the shore. The parallel rule.

That was how we swam, you and me. Parallel to each other. Parallel to the shore. But you are striding away from me now and when I call you do not turn. You spread your arms, dive, surface and begin to swim, each elbow by turns rising gracefully from the sea. Hands curved, you cup the water and push it backwards, your pale head moving further and further away. The sun sparkles. Afternoon drifts away. I turn. The mother has gathered the empty bottles and toys and bags and is heading for her car. A child drags a beach towel behind her. The man with the dog is sitting in a van. The dog is on his shoulder. Gears grind and the van trundles away. And we are alone.

There is a place in town, a parking lot by the sea where people go on stormy days to sit in the warmth of their cars and stare out at the churning sea. The wind would be from the north or worse, the northeast, and people would sit and stare, fishermen, retired fishermen, wives and husbands and daughters and sons and they would think, Thank God we are not out there today. They would sit with their Tim Horton's teas and coffees and shake their heads in wonder at the sea.

But today, today is calm and the breeze is gentle and from the southwest. And I look at you swimming away from me. How many feet now, how many metres? One hundred feet, the length of an Olympic pool? More? How far? How far have you gone, and why have you not turned? And there is in me a dread. I hear this silence, I see this sea, calm, blue, for what it is.

I call your name. But the sea is closing about you. It is too late to scream to the man in the van. The woman with the children. I still see you. A small faint ellipse. As if you have been cut off at the head. And what remains, what is it? Is that you? Is it a ball? A swollen plastic bag? The sea stretches away. It stretches to Newfoundland and Ireland. I squint. It has to be you. Your head weaves like the bubble in a spirit level, this side, that side, centre. This side, that side, centre.

I will you to turn. I will you with all my might to turn around and come back to shore. I remember that this worked before. You were younger then, much younger. We were on the beach then too. You and your little friend James and his sister Rosie. It was six o'clock. The heat still there, but the sun's rays softened. The lifeguards were packed up and leaving. Surfboards locked away. Their lookout chairs empty.

There was a football in the water. An American football, close to shore. The tide was going out and what breeze there was came from the southwest, an offshore breeze. Before I could say a word you were after it. As you swam, the football moved gently beyond your reach. I had not time to warn you. Not time to remind you of the parallel rule. So you swam heedlessly out into the channel and towards the treacherous gut, from which the water was racing in little pulsing dancing waves, playfully toppling the ball. Rosie was too small to leave near the water, James too young to mind her. With Rosie in my arms and James beside me we waded out. We reached a sandbar, waded out further. My blue cotton dress wrapped about my thighs. And we were so quiet. So quiet as we stared at you. At your small head and flagging arms. Willing you back to us. And then you turned. You were almost beside us when I stepped forward and the bar rose up and I said, You can stand. You can stand.

My eyes are fierce now. My whole body is willing you to turn. I do not have that extra power today, of Rosie. And James. This is how it happens. I move out further, searching for a sandbar. I look to the shore but the only movement is a black dog bounding over a sand dune.

Would the girl swim out for him? She would. Even though she had said no to him. Because that was that and this is this. She would not stand and will, knowing nothing about the power of will. She would give scudding kicks and be out there, beside him in minutes. That's how it is with young people now. They can all swim. There are ghosts at my back, tongues lick my cheek.

What would I give now for your passive suffering, your young body safe in your bed?

I am trying not to panic as I think of you under the dying sun. And I start to pray, even though I never pray. But I'll try anything. Will. Prayer. Bargains. A miraculous hand under you before you are overcome with tiredness. I have read those stories. About that tiredness, that wish for nothing more than blissful sleep. And I could have left you, definitely not blissful, but alive in your bed. In that room with the blinds and the walls and the sheet drawn about you. Not out on this wide blue unforgiving sea.

The horizon is long and pale and eye level and falling into water and more water. If I tilt my head back I can still breathe. I take another step and the water is over my head. I swim knowing that if I reach my feet down they will not touch bottom. The water sucks at my mouth. Salt is in my throat. I am ready to drown for you because what else can a mother do? It is too late to look for saving sticks on the beach. There are no life buoys, no bright pink or green noodles left behind by careless children. I turn onto my back to rest for a minute. It was always my breathing that made me such a poor swimmer. It was always too shallow and now it is more shallow. The thought of that vast vast water. It is as though I am swimming up from some deep pit and I know that it is not the water but myself. So contained. So preciously bloody contained. In brine.

I'm sorry, Joey. I was wrong. Will I be able to tell him that?

How long before the sun drops and moonlight pours over the sea? Maybe caught by the edge of a wave the way I was that time out in Kennington Cove and sent scooting up the beach like a wet towel. Salt water streaming from my nose, my ears, leaking from every orifice and a life guard in a tight red suit looming over me, shocked. If I could do that, then I can do this, I think. Otherwise what?

I carefully roll over again and try a side kick but I cannot see you. I turn, using my arms like paddles. I can feel the struggle begin, feel myself losing as I flail against the clutch of the water. And then I see your head, like a seal's, pivoting from side to side. And I know you are looking for me. You start to swim. Towards me.

Mom! Your voice harsh across the water. What are you doing? I breathe in and out, counting to four, holding, releasing. And then you are beside me, laughing the way you always do when you are scared.

Just lie on your back and kick. You say. Kick.

I can feel your hand under my arm, pulling. All those swimming lessons I drove you to on wintry Saturday mornings. Looking at you in amazement as you sliced your way through that thin water. What was the difference between swimming and not swimming? Between swimming and drowning, and I had tried it, it looked so effortless, away from the side railing of the pool, kick, kick, but my legs would droop and I kicked harder but I could not stop that falling deeper and deeper, and the nice young instructor said, after pulling me swiftly to the steps, Perhaps you should stay in the shallow end for a while longer and work on your stroke.

Your grip is firm and together we start to move. A slow, slow movement; my feet like wounded birds barely flicking. Where did the water stop and my skin begin? My legs stretch before me like the limbs of spruce trees too long in the sea. Not smoothed the way rocks and glass are but scaly and soft. I give two more kicks and we collapse together onto the sand. Grains sting my cheek. I reach my hand, white, puckered, towards yours. And stop. And wait. And I'm thinking to myself about this ridiculous vision I have had of myself, swimming on and on and how in the vision I am always a perfect swimmer and the water always holds and enfolds me and how maybe it is time to change. And I'm thinking to myself now too, that maybe I will say yes to Reggie's invitation to a barbecue at his place tonight. He's just put in a new pool. Not one of those in-ground ones that shelve from zero to fifteen in a few yards, well, half a yard actually. No, Reggie has installed an above-ground circular pool that has been newly shocked into a brilliant turquoise and is four foot deep and no deeper. With a little vacuum that hoovers around the bottom of the pool like an underwater dog, cleaning everything in its path. And that's a possibility.

*J*arvis

JULIE CURWIN

*T*HERE ARE NO PORCUPINES ON CAPE BRETON ISLAND. That's one good thing, at least.

When we drove through New Brunswick, there were so many dead porcupines on the side of the road that we started counting them just to entertain ourselves. Twenty-seven by the time we reached Moncton.

I said, "There's some sort of porcupine mass suicide going on in this province."

Roanne said, "Maybe they know something we don't."

Frederick Nietzsche said, "Maybe they've been watching too much CNN."

Margaret said, "Too bad they're not minks or muskrats. We could have made a coat."

None of us had ever seen a live porcupine.

TWO WEEKS AGO my Aunt Darlene called and said, "Jenny, your mother's gone," and I said, "Gone where?" and she said, "Get your sorry arse back to Cape Breton. The funeral is Monday."

I LIVE IN BUILDING NUMBER THREE of the Rowan-Dixon Affordable Housing Complex in the north end of Kingston, Ontario. RD for short. Margaret and Roanne live in the apartment across the hall. They wear three-piece colour-coordinated outfits—shirts, slacks, cardigans—made entirely of sweatpant material. They smoke black-market unfiltered cigarettes, lighting one off the other. The tips of their fingers have turned dark orange. They eat microwave popcorn for breakfast. That's the first thing I smell every morning when I wake up, that sweet buttery aroma drifting across the hall. It's the best time of the day. The rest of the time, this whole sorry apartment complex smells like a dirty sweatsock. The kids at the junior high school across the road say that "RD" stands for "Retards and Druggies." They have spray painted this in tall dripping black letters across the front of Building Number One.

THREE YEARS AGO, the man in the apartment next to mine had his name legally changed to Frederick Nietzsche. He has a sign on his door that says: "We Are the Last Men." Below that there is another sign with a picture of a cat sitting next to a gingerbread house that says: "Welcome Friends."

MY MOTHER CHECKED HERSELF into the Presidential Suite of the Royal Elizabeth Hotel in Sydney, Nova Scotia, for three days, then put the DO NOT DISTURB sign out so she'd be good and dead by the time they discovered her. They found six empty pill bottles on the bedside table and a used Fleet Enema kit in the bathroom. She sure did want to die, my mother, but only, apparently, if she could do so without shitting herself. There was no note. Mom never was sentimental.

EVERY FRIDAY NIGHT for the past two years, Frederick Nietzsche has invited Margaret and Roanne and me over to his place to listen to music and play gin rummy. He calls us his "three tons of fun." Sometimes we order pizza or Chinese food and talk about the decline of Western civilization. Margaret is winning the gin rummy tournament by eleven games.

WHEN I WAS SIX OR SEVEN YEARS OLD, I made up an

imaginary mother. This was the mother I would tell people about—the one who braided my hair with pink ribbons and baked birthday cakes in the shapes of cartoon characters. Not the one who stayed in her dark bedroom all the time and smelled like an ashtray and told me when I cried to shut my mouth or she'd really give me something to cry about. Not the one who was taken away to the hospital for months at a time.

ROANNE WAS A HAIR STYLIST, and a good one too, until her back gave out. She still meets people in the supermarket who say, "Nobody can cut my hair the way you used to, Roanne." Margaret has rheumatoid arthritis and fibromyalgia. She's the same age as me but looks old enough to be my mother. She drinks two litres of Diet Pepsi every day. She is psychic. To make extra money she reads tea leaves and Tarot cards. I'm not the most superstitious person in the world, but I really believe she is psychic. I have my reasons. Sometimes, in the evening, I hear Margaret and Roanne yelling at their TV set. The night my Aunt Darlene called, I heard Margaret yell, "Buy a vowel, for Christ's sake."

FREDERICK NIETZSCHE USED TO BE a tax accountant named Fred MacAllister. He left his office building one day at noon to get some fresh air, when an unspeakably beautiful woman jogged by and he was transfixed by her breasts. Those were his exact words: "She was unspeakably beautiful. I was transfixed." She wore a bra-top that said New Balance in big white letters across the front and he took this as a sign that he needed to change his life.

IN 1975, WHEN I WAS NINE YEARS OLD and my brother Harold was twenty-one, he came into my bedroom one night smelling of beer and said, "I want to show you what brothers and sisters do when they love each other." Mom was in the Nova Scotia Hospital at the time.

THE GOVERNMENT OF ONTARIO considers giving up your job as a tax accountant, changing your name to Frederick Nietzsche, and calling yourself a philosopher, a disability.

DR. DALPINDER SINGH THOMPSON is my psychiatrist. He says that I will have to take lithium for the rest of my life. Lithium is a mood stabilizer, which makes me bland and boring. It makes my skin flaky and my head spacey and I have to pee about a hundred times a day. But I would take rat poison if it prevented me from ending up like my mother.

FREDERICK NIETZSCHE BELIEVES we are living at the end of times. He says that the greatest challenge in life is to be fully conscious of reality, however grim it may be, and still find a way to experience joy in everyday things.

DR. DALPINDER SINGH THOMPSON said we don't get to choose our parents but there's no sense in blaming them for everything. "You inherited your mother's genes, Jennifer," he said, "but you are not your mother." One time I found twenty dollars in the waiting room of his office and he said, "Oh well, finders keepers," but I think he dropped it there on purpose for me to find. I love that man.

FREDERICK NIETZSCHE'S EX-WIFE is a real estate agent, and a successful one at that. She lets him borrow her second car whenever he needs it, which is the least she can do considering the fact he could have taken her for half of everything she's worth, plus monthly alimony payments. What Frederick Nietzsche calls his epiphany, his wife refers to as his breakdown. She is in agreement with the government of Ontario on this.

THE FIRST TIME MARGARET READ MY TEA LEAVES, I thought she was full of shit. She said, "There will be times of great darkness followed by times of great joy," and I said, "Well, Nostradamus, I'm bipolar—you don't have to be psychic to predict that." But the last time I saw her before my mother died, it was spooky. She said, "I see a long journey. I see a casket and something that looks like...needles." Needles? We didn't know what to make of that last part until we drove through New Brunswick. Needles. Porcupine Quills.

FREDERICK NIETZSCHE MAKES UP PAMPHLETS about how to live with courage at the end of times and hands them out in front of the public library. Most people think he's a religious freak, which is sort of funny, because he has a huge poster on his living room wall that says "God Is Dead."

THE LADY AT THE COUNTY WELFARE OFFICE said, "The best we can do is two hundred dollars."

I said, "How am I supposed to get to Cape Breton on that?"

She said, "Maybe your family can help out?"

I said, "Just give me the goddamned two hundred dollars."

When I got home, Margaret and Roanne and Frederick Nietzsche heard me crying and came over to my apartment. Roanne made boiled tea. Margaret massaged my feet. Frederick Nietzsche said, "Jenny, honey, if getting to Cape Breton is the problem, don't worry, I'll drive you. Margaret and Roanne can come along too, if they like. It will be an adventure."

WHEN I WAS TWELVE YEARS OLD, I told two people what my brother Harold was doing to me at night—my mother and our parish priest, Father Paul Ibbotsen. Mom told me to stop telling lies. Father Ibbotsen said that God would forgive me, that God forgives all things. Up until then, I wasn't aware that I'd done anything that needed God's forgiveness. I just wanted Harold to stop.

WE ADDED UP OUR FUNDS for the trip: Margaret had one hundred and seventy-eight dollars she had earned at the Psychic Fair the previous week. I had the two-hundred-dollar cheque from the welfare office. Roanne sold half of her clonazepam and eight of her twenty-milligram Oxycontin tablets to the drug dealer upstairs for one hundred and fifty dollars. Frederick Nietzsche had a silver 2002 Honda Civic with a full tank of gas and fifteen dollars in cash. Roanne made tuna-fish sandwiches. I baked a double batch of oatmeal raisin cookies. Margaret supplied two cases of Diet Pepsi she had stockpiled when they were half price at SuperSaver. Frederick Nietzsche's ex-wife left a bag of groceries in the back of the car which contained five packages of goat's-milk cheese with peppercorns, one double variety pack of stoned wheat crackers, and three magnum bottles of 2005 Australian Cabernet Sauvignon. "She was probably on her way to an open house and forgot which car it was in," he said, "but I'm going to think of it as a gift."

IN 2005, FATHER PAUL IBBOTSEN was found guilty of child molestation and sentenced to six years in prison. Most of his crimes had taken place back in the '60s and '70s. He had a preference for pre-pubescent altar boys. Like my brother Harold.

AFTER WE'D FINISHED PACKING THE CAR, Frederick Nietzsche got his camera out and asked a passer-by to take our picture. We must have seemed like a strange crew—Frederick Nietzsche standing there, small as a gnat, head too big for his tiny body and ears sticking out at right angles, three women the size of beluga whales huddled around him. He looked like he could disappear inside the cleft under Margaret's breasts and never find his way out.

DR. DALPINDER SINGH THOMPSON was the first doctor to diagnose me correctly. Bipolar Affective Disorder. BAD. I'm a BAD BAD girl. Manic-Depression is what they used to call it, back when people still used accurate language. The manic part isn't so bad. Sure, you might wreck your life—spend all your money, sleep with people you shouldn't sleep with, tell your boss to fuck off—that sort of thing, but there is no other feeling in the world that even comes close to it. It's like having an orgasm that lasts for two weeks straight. It's like kissing Johnny Depp, *with* tongue. I can understand why Mom kept going off her lithium. She was trying to recapture that high. I'm tempted myself, sometimes. The problem is, you can't stay manic. It's as if you use up all your happy brain chemicals at once and then you crash like a skydiver who forgot to pack a parachute. The depression part of Manic-Depression, as my dead mother can attest, is no fun at all.

I HAVE A PICTURE IN A FIVE-BY-SEVEN FRAME that I keep beside my bed. I am about four years old, standing between my mother and my brother, wearing a bright orange cape and black leotards. I look like a pumpkin. Mom's hair is long. She's wearing a beaded headband and a white mini-dress. Harold has curly blond hair and is looking away from the camera. We are all smiling. I try to recall who was holding the camera, but I can't remember anything about that day. It must have been before Mom's illness got really bad. She looked so pretty then. Such a kind face. The woman in that picture might have baked me a birthday cake in the shape of a cartoon character.

ON SATURDAY MORNING, we started down Division Street and onto the 401 East, towards Quebec. Frederick Nietzsche put the driver's seat all the way forward and even then he could hardly reach the gas pedal. He drove slowly, transport trucks roaring past us one after the other: President's Choice; Coca-Cola; Allied Van Lines; McDonald's. We were not in a hurry. We stopped for the night just outside Riviere-du-Loup, at a motel that advertised

"XXX Danseuses SuperSexy!!" on a tall neon sign. Dayglo pink breasts blinked on and off. The only other patrons, judging by the contents of the parking lot, were four long-haul truckers and a decent-sized motorcycle gang.

Margaret said, "Why are we stopping here?"

Frederick Nietzsche said, "Aren't we supposed to be having an adventure?"

Roanne said, "I've always wanted to go to a strip joint."

I said, "I don't care where we stop as long as it's cheap and doesn't have bedbugs."

Roanne said, "Well, it is cheap."

After we checked in, I ate goat's-milk cheese with peppercorns for the first time in my life.

TWO YEARS AGO, my brother Harold put a .22-calibre hunting rifle in his mouth and pulled the trigger. He aimed upward. If there's one thing my fucked-up family seems to be good at, it's killing ourselves. I mailed a copy of Harold's obituary to Father Paul Ibbotsen, c/o Dorchester Penitentiary. On the back of it I wrote: Dear Father, Does God really forgive *all* things?

ASIDE FROM COUNTING DEAD PORCUPINES—twenty-seven—I don't remember much about New Brunswick, but when we crossed the border into Nova Scotia, I felt my stomach getting queer. Margaret reached up from the back seat and put her hand on my shoulder.

"My mother's dead," I said.

"I know," she said.

THIS IS FREDERICK NIETZSCHE'S MANTRA, which he borrowed from the German poet, Rainer Maria von Rilke: Dennoch Preisen. To praise in spite of. One night in the middle of a game of gin rummy he told me, "God is dead, Jenny, that's true, but everything, and I mean everything, is sacred."

CROSSING THE CANSO CAUSEWAY wasn't as traumatic as I thought it would be but that's because Roanne, bless her morbidly obese soul, started feeding me nerve pills just outside Antigonish. There is no grief so terrible that it can't be numbed out with enough clonazepam. When I read the sign that said *Welcome to Cape Breton*, I actually giggled.

I DON'T REMEMBER MUCH about the funeral itself. Somebody had dressed Mom in a silky light blue dress with puffy sleeves. It reminded me of something a perky 1980s bridesmaid might have worn. I leaned over to Frederick Nietzsche and said, "Mom wouldn't have been caught dead in that."

MY IMAGINARY MOTHER worked as a hair stylist to the stars. I told Roanne this while she was doing my hair for the funeral, and she laughed so hard that her back went into spasms and she had to sit down.

AT THE RECEPTION AFTER THE FUNERAL, I ate egg salad sandwiches and oatcakes while people came up to me and said, "You know, dear, your mother was just never the same after Harold...." That's how every single one of them finished—or rather, didn't finish—their sentence: "after Harold...."

"After Harold what?" I wanted to ask. "Sprayed his brain matter across the walls and ceiling of the Motel Six? Gave up, like the pathetic chicken-shit alcoholic that he was, and took the easy way out?"

But the sentence non-completers weren't half as bad as the well-intentioned morons who took me by the hand and said things like, "She's in a better place now" or "She's finally at peace." It was only Roanne's clonazepam—washed down with liberal quantities of Frederick Nietzsche's ex-wife's red wine—that got me through that ordeal, nodding solemnly in the direction of each moron and saying "Thank you, you're so kind," when what I really wanted to do was to knock their teeth out. Why couldn't just one person be honest and say something like: "Your mother was a rotten, selfish bitch to leave you like that, with no explanation, and never once having baked you a birthday cake in the shape of a cartoon character."

THERE IS AT LEAST ONE LIVING PORCUPINE in New Brunswick. He resides at the Pleasant Hill Game Farm just outside Fredericton. His name is Jarvis and, as far as I can tell, he just sits there on a tree branch all day like a giant prickly slug. But he *is* alive. This much I know because Margaret said she saw his eyes move. The lady at the ticket booth looked surprised when the first question we asked was: "Which way to the porcupine?"

"Don't you want to see the baby moose?" she asked.

WHEN WE GOT BACK TO KINGSTON, I told Dr. Dalpinder Singh Thompson that I felt lost, that nothing seemed certain anymore, so he gave me what he called a grounding exercise. He said: Write down five things that you do know. Here's what I've come up with so far:

I know that my mother is dead—along with God, my brother Harold, and about ten thousand New Brunswick porcupines.

I know that not every porcupine in this world is a dead porcupine—although you do have to go out of your way to find one that's alive.

I know that everything, and I mean everything, is sacred.

I know who my friends are.

I know that I am not my mother.

MY BIRTHDAY WAS TWO DAYS AGO. Roanne and Margaret baked me a cake. It had an odd oblong shape and was covered with chocolate icing and short pieces of brown shoe-string licorice. It took me a minute to recognize it as Jarvis the porcupine. Not exactly a cartoon character, but I'll take it.

*H*er *T*op *F*orty

NANCY S. M. WALDMAN

"**W**HAT'S NUMBER FORTY?" I ASKED, trying to distract her.

She couldn't answer for a moment, her breath lost to the high altitude. "*She Lives in a...Time of her Own*, 13th Floor Elevators," she finally said, and I just knew we'd be okay.

Joyce hired me over a year ago to do her yard work. My mom set the whole thing up. "She's got MS, Colin," Mom told me, "so always ask if there's anything else you can do for her." Turns out, Joyce didn't have a problem asking for what she needed. I'd get things off shelves, change light bulbs, lift heavy stuff. It had always been small favours until the other day.

"Colin," she said, looking out her kitchen window toward Mt. Henley, "I want to go to the top of the mountain. Would you take me?"

"Um. Sure. I guess."

"It's one thing I must do before I die."

"You're going to die?"

She laughed. "Yes. Aren't you?"

I didn't laugh, so she quickly told me that she didn't know when she would die and that people with her kind of multiple sclerosis live almost as long as people who don't have it. I tuned her out, trying to think of a good excuse not to take her. I liked her okay, but I didn't want to spend a day in the car with her.

"You can't drive there?" I asked.

"Nooo. Hell, I get dizzy on flat roads."

Which begs the question, Why go up a mountain?

"NUMBER THIRTY-TWO?"

"*Ladies of the...Canyon*, Joni Mitchell." Then, several deep breaths later, "Thirty-one...Soundgarden, *Black Hole Sun*."

JOYCE HAD A KICK-ASS VINYL COLLECTION, an astounding digital music collection, and she knew absolutely everything about music. I felt shy talking to her at first, but then every time I went in her house, she had on Radiohead or Pink Floyd or someone amazing I'd never heard of. She also had a shiny, vintage Harley in her garage.

"It belonged to my ex-husband. He's been gone a long time." Joyce sighed. "Those were fandamnedtastic times. Like it?"

"It's awesome. My dad had one." I couldn't believe that came out of my mouth. I never saw or talked about my dad. He left my mom a year ago. For a man.

How messed up is that?

"WHAT...ARE...WE UP...TO?"

"Five, Joyce. Almost there." Twenty through Ten had all been mountain songs. *Rocky Mountain High, Your Love Keeps Lifting Me Higher, Climb Every Mountain*. We laughed a lot, which slowed her down and made her cough. It also kept us going.

"Five's...gotta be...*Bird on a Wire*."

"Leonard Cohen," I said for her. "Why not *Suzanne*?" She didn't bother answering.

"HERE WE ARE," I SAID, when we had finally arrived in the Mt. Henley parking area.

"What?" Joyce asked, her voice sharp. "This is as far as we can go?"

"There are look-off points. Got your binocs?"

"But Colin, we aren't at the summit."

"Close enough."

"I need to go to the very top."

She's disappointed? That really takes nerve. Joyce never ran out of that particular commodity, which is pretty ironic considering her illness has something to do with her nerves not being healthy. "Joyce, please. Would you look at the damned view!"

"There must be a trail."

"Maybe. I suppose," I said, looking around. "Yeah. The trail head's over there."

"Have you been?"

"No."

"Then we must do it. For you."

"For me? Yeah, right."

"You'll see. It'll be good."

"You can barely walk through your living room without falling! No. No!"

"Boy, listen to me. I do three impossible things before breakfast every—damned—day."

Argue with Joyce? Why bother? "I'll go see what it's like while you get ready."

I returned to find her leaning on her cane, already short of breath. "Joyce," I said, feeling a little breathless myself, "it's not wheelchair accessible. But, if you can get to the first look-off"—I pointed to it and she nodded, her hat brim flopping—"it's only forty more steps. Maybe we could do a 'best songs' countdown. To keep your mind occupied."

Twenty minutes later at the look-off, Joyce sat, recuperating. "Open the backpack," she said. Inside was a canister of oxygen. I hooked it up at her instructions and she clipped the catheter into her nostrils.

It took Joyce way more than forty steps, but every five or so,

I played DJ. On any other day, I knew, her song list would be different.

"Number Two," I shouted, so happy to be close to the top.

She took a long, long time to answer. *"Piece...My Heart*, Ragovoy and Berns."

Leave it to Joyce to know who wrote it. "Janis Joplin," I said, proud to know anything.

"First...recorded by Erma Franklin, Aretha's sister," she said. "Though Janis...*whew*. Amazing."

I held out my hand to her. "You made it."

She grimaced, pulling up the last step. "We made it." Turning in a slow circle, breathing deeply, she said, "You...choose the last song."

"No. You." I wanted to hear what she'd dredge up out of that brain of hers.

"Okay then...the Number One song...in Joyce's Top Forty: *Father and Son* by Cat Stevens." She looked up at me. "You are going to be fine, you know."

"Forty impossible things before supper," I said, voice cracking.

She held onto me for balance and, together, we took in the view from the top.

The Writers

Russell Colman was born and raised in the Chicago area. Retired after a 22-year career as a logistics officer in the US Marine Corps, he now lives in Cape Breton. He's a member of the Writers' Federation of Nova Scotia. In 2008 he was short-listed for the Debut Dagger Award by the Crime Writers Association. This is his first published work.

Bill Conall grew up in Ontario and lived for several years each in Saskatoon and British Columbia, before moving to Cape Breton for good. He spent seven years on the road as a musician and twelve more as a long-haul trucker. Now he writes, goes fishing, plays darts, and cuts his own firewood. His first book, *The Rock in the Water*, was shortlisted for the 2010 Stephen Leacock Award for Humour.

Julie Curwin is a psychiatrist who divides her time between Sydney and Boulard018derie, where she lives with her husband and a motley assortment of feline friends. Her short story "World Backwards" was the overall winner of the Commonwealth Short Story Competition in 2008-09. "Jarvis" won a Writers' Federation of New Brunswick short fiction competition.

Born in Ingonish, Cape Breton Island, **Stewart Donovan** is the author of two books of poetry and the novel, *Maritime Union*. His biography of R. J. MacSween, *The Forgotten World*, was short-listed for the Atlantic Non-Fiction Awards. A professor at St. Thomas University, Stewart is the founder of the Irish Studies Program and the Film and Media Studies Major. He edits *The Nashwaak Review*.

Dave Doucette is the author of *Strong at the Broken Places*, winner of the Dartmouth Book Award for fiction, and *North of Smokey*. His stories have appeared in *Pottersfield Portfolio*, *Nashwaak Review*, *Hiroshima Signpost* (Japan), and the *Telegraph Journal*. Dave divides his time between his native Ingonish, and the rest of the world. He is now teaching in Qatar.

Born in 1948 and a graduate of Queen's University and St Lawrence College, **Larry Gibbons** is a former library clerk, photo technologist, and veterinary technologist. A book lover, enthusiastic hiker, and passionate writer, he spends as much time as he can in Cape Breton Island. When in Ontario, Larry and his wife live in a cabin in the woods. His collection of sixteen stories, *White Eyes*, has been published by Breton Books.

Maureen Hull was born and raised on Cape Breton Island, and educated at Dalhousie University, Nova Scotia College of Art and Design, and the Pictou Fisheries

School. Since 1976 she has lived on a small island in the Northumberland Strait. She is the author of several books for adults and for children, and recently served as the Pictou-Antigonish Regional Library Writer-in-Residence.

A journalist since 1980, **Phonse Jessome** has received regional and national awards, including (AJ's) Atlantic Journalism awards, (RTNDA) Radio Television News Directors Association awards, and (CAB) Canadian Association of Broadcasters awards. Having covered crime all over Nova Scotia, he is the author of the bestselling non-fiction books, *Murder at McDonalds* and *Somebody's Daughter*.

Frank Macdonald is an award-winning newspaper columnist and a novelist. His publications include novels *A Forest for Calum* (2005), long-listed for the 2007 IM-PAC International Dublin Literary Award, and *A Possible Madness* (2011). He and his partner, artist-illustrator Virginia McCoy, have co-written a children's novella, *T.R.'s Adventure at Angus the Wheeler's*. Frank lives in Inverness.

Angus MacDougall is a native of Sydney Mines. He currently divides his time between Richmond County and Kempt Head, Victoria County. Several of his earlier stories were published in *The Antigonish Review*. He served briefly as an assistant chaplain with the RCAF and was commissioned as a Pilot Officer in 1965.

Paul MacDougall, an instructor in Health Studies at Cape Breton University, writes and publishes fiction and non-fiction, and is a longtime member of the local CBC Radio Book Panel. With Ken Chisholm, he has written five award-winning one-act plays. He is the author of the best-selling *Distinction Earned: Cape Breton Boxing Legends, 1946-1970*. He lives in Sydney with his wife Faye and son Samuel.

Teresa O'Brien was born in Ireland and now lives in Glace Bay. Her work has been anthologised in English, Canadian, and American literary journals. Her first collection of short stories, *The Keys*, was published in 2010 by Breton Books. She has written stories that will soon appear in *The Windsor Review* and *The New Writer*.

Born in Judique, **Joyce Rankin** saw her book of poetry, *At My Mother's Door*, go into a rare third printing, and become a play that toured Cape Breton and was included in a multimedia exhibition that toured Scotland and Nova Scotia. Enroute to her first novel, she works for Habitat for Humanity and Cape Breton University.

Victor Sakalauskas has published two stories and is working on a novel that takes place in Cape Breton. He lives in New Minas, Nova Scotia.

D. C. Troicuk's work has appeared in *Canadian Living, The Antigonish Review, Pottersfield Portfolio, Gaspereau Review, The Nashwaak Review*, and in several anthologies. Her short story collection, *Loose Pearls*, was published by Cape Breton University Press.

Brian Tucker was born in New Waterford, Cape Breton. His first novel, *Big White Knuckles*, was shortlisted for the Amazon.ca First Novel Award and the Re-lit Award. Brian currently resides in Miramichi, New Brunswick, with his wife and three children. He is at work on his second novel. "The Drunk Tank" is an excerpt from that novel.

Tim Vassallo is the author of short stories, one-act plays, and a feature-length screenplay. His work reflects growing up in the Ashby neighbourhood of Sydney as well as ancestral lore that reaches back to the settlement of Big Pond. Tim developed and taught the "Writing in the Margins" creative writing program for at-risk youth. He is finishing his first novel.

Nancy S. M. Waldman writes short stories and novels. She is co-founder and editor with Third Person Press which specializes in publishing regional authors of speculative fiction. Her work has been published in *The Nashwaak Review* and in two anthologies: *Undercurrents* and *Airborne*. She grew up in Texas but happily transplanted to Cape Breton over ten years ago.

In the making of this book, we have lost contact with **Mary Steele** (Mary MacIntyre), author of "Mira Milk Run," and would appreciate word from or about her.

ALSO AVAILABLE FROM
Breton Books

Song of Rita Joe
Autobiography of a Mi'kmaw Poet
by RITA JOE

IN THIS CANADIAN CLASSIC, Rita Joe leaves us her story of poverty, sheer guts and compassion. She fought her gentle war for family, justice, and her own independent voice—emerging as an honoured Elder, poet, and member of the Order of Canada. It has been called a "heart-wrenching and triumphal autobiography"—Prof. A. LaVonne Brown Rouoff.

202 PAGES • PHOTOS • ISBN 978-1-926908-04-5

Sister to Courage
Stories from the World of Viola Desmond, Canada's Rosa Parks
by WANDA ROBSON

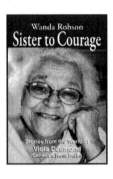

BELOVED STORYTELLER Wanda Robson is a sister of Viola Desmond, civil rights icon and African-Nova Scotian businesswoman. Through touching and hilarious stories, Wanda shares the roots of courage, ambition, good fun and dignity of the household that produced Viola. Here Viola shines through, beyond the moment she defied the racist rules of a New Glasgow movie theatre. An insightful look into a unique family, **Sister to Courage** keeps important history alive. It includes the Nova Scotia Apology and Royal Grant of Free Pardon of Viola Desmond.

184 PAGES, PHOTOGRAPHS • ISBN 978-1-895415-34-6

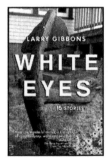

WHITE EYES
16 Stories
by LARRY GIBBONS

WELCOME TO THE WORLD of Larry Gibbons. Brought to a Mi'kmaw First Nation reserve by a woman's love, and privileged to live there for ten years, Gibbons has written a rare and extraordinary batch of short stories. Sometimes he gets it right. Often he is the confused white man. But story by story, he delivers terrific reading—compassionate, often comic and absolutely unique.

176 PAGES • ISBN 978-1-926908-07-6

The Woman from Away
THE COLLECTED WRITING OF CAPE BRETON'S
TESSIE GILLIS

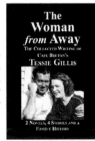

THE GODMOTHER OF CAPE BRETON FICTION, Tessie's sharp, compassionate eye transmuted characters shaped by hard work, alcohol, and intense community bonds into a captivating, real, vibrant portrait—the very heart of Cape Breton. Here are her novels, remarkable short stories, and more. No one has ever written about Cape Breton quite like this.

288 PAGES • 978-1-895415-92-6

Breton Books
Wreck Cove, Cape Breton, Nova Scotia B0C 1H0
bretonbooks@ns.sympatico.ca • 1-800-565-5140
www.capebretonbooks.com